JENIFER WOOD

Cover art by Rowan Woodcock

Cover design by Ash Raven

Editing by Alex Yuschik and Emily Michel

ISBN: 979-8-9879953-8-9 [Ebook]

ISBN: 979-8-9879953-9-6 [Paperback]

Piracy is a major issue for indie authors like me, who invest countless hours into our books. It directly impacts our ability to support ourselves and keep creating new work.

If you know someone who would enjoy this book but can't access it through legal means, please contact me at authorjeniferwood@gmail.com. If you're currently reading a pirated copy, I'd appreciate hearing from you as well. I'm committed to finding a way to get my book into readers' hands legally.

Thank you for your support and understanding.

A NOTE ABOUT CONTENT

I am a lazy reader and used to never read the content warnings. And then I realized I am also an *anxious* reader and would love a heads-up if things are about to get dark. This series is relatively light but I want to be sensitive to all readers. So, you can view this as a content warning, or you can view this as a menu.

Either way, *spoilers ahead.*

- Spousal abuse (off page)
- Parental abuse (off page)
- Religious trauma
- Drugging
- Kidnapping
- Explicit sexual scenes
- Knotting
- Stretching and stuffing
- On page violence (minor)
- Pregnancy

If you have any specific content you are concerned about, you are welcome to reach out to me at authorjeniferwood@gmail.com.

To all the youth group dropouts.

CHAPTER 1

TRACY

Tuesday night, all the girls decided to get all dressed up and head to the local bar. I'd worked at Coco's for almost a month and was finally starting to feel comfortable in San Diego. I had no fear of Gabe finding me. I had a steady job and a cozy place to live, even if it was always a mess. I'd made a solid group of girlfriends at my hostess job. When I'd showed up at a motel with a black eye and fifty-two dollars to my name, Trish helped me find work. She wasn't the warmest, but she saw a girl in need and stepped in. She helped me get the job at Coco's. One night, as I returned to the motel, Trish offered me her old roommate's room—she was moving in with her boyfriend. As prickly as Trish was, I didn't hesitate.

That's how I ended up in a worn-down bungalow right on the ocean on the outskirts of San Diego.

I'd had to borrow clubbing clothes from Stacy, since, having fled from Gabe when I saw my chance, I didn't have time to pack much. And given my former life, I definitely didn't have clubbing clothes. My parents raised me in a high-control cult on the outskirts of Boulder. If Gabe, technically still my husband, understood me at all, he'd know that I had not only fled our small town, but I had fled the state—on an Amtrak. Yet, he was dumb as a pile of rocks, so I wouldn't be surprised if he were currently scandalizing the small community I grew up in by trying to find me in the neighboring towns. Now, over a thousand miles away, the past felt like a separate country. I was determined to leave it there. Here, with Trish and my girls, I felt safe for the first time in a long time.

I looked at myself in the mirror. I was in an electric pink dress far shorter than I would have picked out for myself and black kitten heels. I had to acknowledge I looked cute, even if it didn't feel *me*. I'd never owned a dress that didn't go to my ankles. This pink, slinky thing highlighted all of my assets, which was new to me. I felt hot and uncertain at the same time.

"It's perfect," Heather squealed, clapping her hands together.

Heather was twenty-one and a ball of energy. She was the ringleader of our little crew. Steph was the oldest and volunteered to stay sober even though we all lived within walking distance of the club. I put my ID, cash, and a tube of lipstick in a clutch I'd borrowed from Heather and was ready to go. The walk was short, and it was late August. The air was balmy and comforting. I could get used to summers in San Diego.

At the club, the bouncer carefully checked all of our IDs. I didn't blame him. We all looked right on the edge of twenty-one. I had turned twenty-two in April. Only when I started making new friends did I learn getting married at twenty was *not* the norm.

We headed into the bar with the sounds of "Material Girl" blaring all around us. At least they had good music. We grabbed one of the tall circular tables near the dance floor while Heather got us three cheap wine coolers and a Diet Coke for Steph. The club was busy for a Tuesday, but it was ladies' night. All our drinks were half off. This ensured that plenty of women *and* men showed up. But I wasn't on the market. I was just there to have fun with my girls. I didn't know when I'd be ready to date again, but it wasn't tonight.

I took another sip of my drink and enjoyed the slight tipsy feeling I was starting to get. I was a complete light-weight, mainly due to having minimal experience drinking. Not only did Gabe disapprove of it, but our church also maligned alcohol. I always wondered what that meant since the Bible had stories of Jesus turning water into wine—but I was too afraid to ask. As that thought flitted across my mind, I took another big sip. Gabe wasn't here. I was free. I could do whatever I wanted.

Three wine coolers later, and we were dancing our hearts out on the dance floor. While I hadn't told any of the girls the sordid details of my past, they knew I'd fled from my ex and had no interest in being found. They were aggressively deflecting any male attention, and I appreciated it immensely. I was drunk but still coherent and having more fun than I'd had in almost a year.

But I needed to pee, so I grabbed Steph's hand. "Come to the bathroom with me?" I asked.

"Sure," she said, heading with me to the bathrooms at the back of the bar. "I'll wait outside for you and make sure no one creepy goes in."

I gave her a sloppy, drunk hug. "Thanks, Steph."

I headed in and did my business in the dimly lit restroom and was finishing up when the lights went out. I was plunged into complete darkness. I screamed and heard shouts come from all around me as if the entire club had been plunged into a bad slasher film. I took a deep breath. *There must be a power outage.* I wiped and pulled my dress down, not bothering with flushing or washing my hands. I needed to find my friends. As much as I didn't want to put my hands all over the bathroom walls, I needed to use them to help me find the door. I reached out in front of me for anything solid to help me get oriented. Finally, after taking a few blind steps, I found the wall and started walking toward what I hoped was the exit. The screaming had stopped, and it had gone eerily quiet.

Before I could get to the door, I heard it creak open. It was still pitch black.

"Steph?" I asked.

No response. I sensed there was someone in the bathroom and started to panic.

"Steph? Heather! STACY?!" I cried into the silence, but no one answered.

As I started to lose it completely, an icy hand with long fingers wrapped around my wrist. I tried to wrench back, but the hand was stronger, and I was pretty drunk. Whatever it was pulled me closer. I struggled and screamed and then felt something cold press against the side of my neck. The darkness closed in on me, and my mind went blank.

CHAPTER 2

FENRIK

I ran down the path out of our tribe at full speed. I didn't know how many would come after me, but I wasn't taking any chances. I would run all night if I had to. I couldn't risk whatever they would do to me if they caught me. I didn't know the punishment for refusing to take the jarl's daughter as a mate, but I wasn't about to find out. Jarl Gorm was a fierce warrior with a vindictive streak. The last time someone questioned his decision about refusing to trade with another tribe, he exiled them, saying if they trusted other tribes more, they might as well go join them.

The punishment for rejecting his daughter would be far worse.

I ran into the night, eating up the miles, but I eventually had to acknowledge I needed shelter. Snaerfire was isolated, up above the tree line, but had a few outposts scattered for hunters to seek refuge in, should they get caught in a storm or go on a several-day hunt. I hadn't been to an outpost since

I had first joined the hunters, but if I remembered correctly, there was one due west. Getting there would take me at least another hour, but it was my safest option.

My steps slowed and my heart rate lowered. With a plan, I could channel my energy in the right direction. I was a hunter. Already, I'd passed beyond where the tribe would continue to look for me. There was no one who knew this area better than me, and it was too cold to search all night.

I walked, following the rough direction I knew the cabin to be, hoping my árs-old memory wouldn't lead me astray. I walked and walked, my feet growing sluggish and my hands going numb with the cold. I had been out and exposed to the elements for hours. It wasn't the cold season yet, but this high up in the mountains, the temperature plummeted when the sun went down. I continued, but I was losing my strength the longer I walked. I almost gave up when I saw the cabin rising in the distance. I used my last bit of energy to sprint flat out.

The door wasn't locked. It was designed for anyone's use, and only our tribe came this high up into the mountains, but it was pitch black inside. I walked in slowly, with my hands outstretched. Using my hands, I skimmed the wall until I found the fireplace. Kneeling in front of the fire place with the fire starter, I struck it, hoping for the best. After several attempts, I was rewarded with a tiny, fragile flame, barely enough to show me the inside of the cabin. But it gave me enough light to see the logs stacked neatly beside the fire.

I set to work building the fire, hands shaking from the numbness and the cold. I was so grateful to find significant refuge at that—my heart clenched. As the fire roared to life, my fingers ached while the feeling returned to them, but that was a good sign. I knelt before the fire, hands raised to it, trying to absorb all the warmth I could.

Eventually, I stood, feeling weak, and looked around the

cabin. It was larger than I remembered, equipped with a full kitchen, a dusty couch, and a dining table. I peered into one of the rooms to find a large, sagging bed. The bedroom had a second fireplace that I would need to build up to stay warm through the night. The other door opened into a small washroom with a sink and a toilet due to the attention of previous generations. This was much better than I could have anticipated.

I sat down on the dusty couch and stared into the fire. Though warm and comfortable now, I couldn't stay in the cabin forever. Eventually, the tribe would realize it was occupied.

The whole situation was a mess. I had nothing against Kelda but didn't want to be her mate. And I definitely didn't want to be mated to the jarl's daughter. The very thought of that kind of expectation made me feel ill. I had no interest in politics. Jarl Gorm wanted me to marry Kelda so that one day we could rule the tribe together.

But I was a hunter. I wanted a simple life. I wanted to find a mate, have a few orklings, and live peacefully in the mountains. I rolled around the permanency of my decision to run from Snaerfire in my head. What if I had just given up any opportunity to have a mate? A permanent home? Kelda wasn't my Elska mate, but she wasn't bad to look at. I didn't care for how she treated the tribe, as if she was above us all. I could never feel comfortable in that kind of relationship. By publicly humiliating her and turning her down, had I just destined my life to one of solitude, traversing from outpost to outpost, living out my days in silence?

I put my head in my hands. A lifetime alone sounded almost as terrible as a lifetime mated to Kelda. I stared into the flames as the minutes ticked by. I tried to think of other options. Joining any of the different tribes was out of the question. They weren't to be trusted. I doubted they would even take me in, considering how we'd treated all of their peacekeeping envoys in the past.

Gorm trusted no orkin outside of Snaerfire.

I let out a sigh and stood. I couldn't solve this tonight. Maybe some sleep would help me come up with new options. I took the fire starter and some wood into the small bedroom and got the fire going nice and large—large enough to last most of the night. I removed my cloak and hung it by the door before removing my boots. It was too cold to take off any of my other layers, so I climbed into the cold bed, wishing the warmth from the fire would spread faster.

I couldn't find sleep for a long time. I tossed and turned, catastrophizing about how Gorm would react when he realized I had no intention of returning or taking Kelda as my mate. I wouldn't be surprised if he wanted to kill me with his bare hands. After what felt like ages, I warmed up and drifted into a fretful sleep.

I dreamt that there was a large light overhead, brighter than the moon, shining down on the little cabin. I had never seen anything like it. It was blinding, coming through every window and crack in the walls. I tried to shield my eyes, but the light came through all the same. I jerked awake and realized the light wasn't in my dream. It was outside the cabin. There was no way anyone from our tribe could make a light like that—we relied on gas and oil lamps when available—and torches when not. I got out of bed and attempted to peer out the window without being seen.

The clearing in front of the cabin was lit up even brighter than I could imagine. A large silver disk floated above the trees, almost blocking the entire night sky. The beam was coming from the disk. I looked to see where it was focused, and there, in the middle of the clearing, lay a small, limp figure. As I tried to figure out what it was, the silver disc shot straight upward, taking its light, and sped off into the night sky. With the disk gone, I could barely make out the clearing before me, let alone whatever had been illuminated. What the hell had I just witnessed?

I ran to the kitchen, shuffled through the cupboards, and was grateful to find a dusty oil lamp. It looked as if it hadn't been used for several seasons, but there was still oil in it. I decided to give it a go and was rewarded with a tiny flicker of a flame. I grabbed my cloak and headed out to the clearing. The night was pitch black, with no moon to speak of. It took me a moment to find what I'd seen, and when I finally did, I had no idea what to make of it.

There it was, crumpled on the ground, still and tiny. It looked kind of like an orc, but only in the most basic way. It had two arms, two legs, and a head with long yellow hair cascading over its face. But that was where the similarities ended. It was much smaller than any orkin I'd seen, and its skin wasn't our usual green—it was a creamy color. And way too much of it was exposed for comfort out in the cold.

I nudged it with my toe, half expecting it to jump up and attack. Nothing. So, I crouched down to get a better look. As I examined it, I realized I had to stop thinking of it as an "it" —whatever it was, it was someone. Their skin was freezing to the touch.

Throwing caution to the wind, I scooped them up and hurried back to the cabin. They needed to get warm. Cold skin wasn't a good sign, regardless of where they'd come from. I pulled them close, using my body heat to protect them. I looked down at their face as I rushed back and realized whatever I was carrying was female. Her face was similar to an orkin's, with two eyes, a nose, and a mouth, but her features were delicate and soft. Light brown lashes fanned out below her closed eyes and her tiny pink mouth hung open. Whatever she was, she was beautiful. Her tiny tunic was a blinding shade of pink I had never seen on Niflheim and was skin-tight, revealing subtle feminine curves. She had the smallest satchel I'd ever seen hooked over her shoulder. I pulled her delicate limbs closer to me, trying to provide all the warmth that I could.

I took her into the small bedroom and wrapped her up in the blankets of the bed. I placed her bag on the floor by the bed before adding logs to the fire. I used all of them to get the fire blazing. I could chop more in the morning. Once I got the fire underway, I checked on her again. I attempted to rearrange the blankets to get her bundled even tighter. I wrapped her up in as many blankets as I could, trying to think if there was any other way to get her warm. This was the best I could offer, so it would have to do. I placed my hand on her forehead and was pleased to feel her skin warming up. I sat down on the dusty armchair next to the bed and decided to keep watch. While I was worried for my own safety, this small fragile female was now relying on me. There was nothing I could do for her until she stirred.

CHAPTER 3

FENRIK

I must have dozed off in the night because I jerked awake to find myself in the early light of pre-dawn. The fire had dwindled and the room chilled. I stood and rushed to the creature I'd found in the night. She wasn't in the same position I had left her in. At some point in the night, she had rolled onto her side and curled up in a ball. I cringed, realizing that probably meant she was still cold, but was also grateful for the sign of life.

I looked her over. Her small mouth was still hanging open, and I could tell she was breathing. I wondered what other signs of life she might have in common with an orc. I thought about checking if her heart was beating but then I stopped to consider whether or not she had a heart. This had to be the most confusing situation I had ever experienced. I wanted to ensure her safety, but I didn't want to scare her. I squatted next to the bed and could see her eyes flickering back and forth under her lids.

I wavered back and forth as I examined her up close. I'd never discovered... I didn't really know what. She wasn't from Niflheim, and I had no idea what to do. I didn't know if there was a protocol for what to do with a creature that appeared in a circle of light in the middle of the woods. This was far out of my area of expertise as a hunter. Given I was so much larger than her and likely looked very foreign to her, I didn't want her to run screaming the minute I woke her. I looked at her closely. A small scattering of light brown dots peppered the bridge of her nose. They were adorable.

Finally, realizing I'd have to go hunt for food at some point, I decided to wake her. I'd rather she wake up with me in the cabin than wake up alone and go wandering out into the cold looking for help.

I brushed a hand across her shoulder, pleased to find her skin warm to the touch. I shook her gently. She shifted and groaned, rolling onto her back. She blinked a couple of times as she came to. She propped herself up on her elbows, continuing to look around when she finally met my gaze.

"Wha—what are you?" she asked.

Surprised to find I could understand her, I responded, "I'm an orc, what are you?"

"I'm a human." She looked very alarmed.

"I've never met a human before. Do you know how you got here?"

"Do *I* know how I got here? Shouldn't I be asking you that? You're the one who attacked me in the club!" Her face screwed up in anger.

I tried to remain calm. After what I had already been through, I didn't need to be accused of attacking someone.

"I didn't attack you in a club," I said, raising my hands to show I meant no harm. "I don't even know what a club is."

"I was in the club, in the bathroom. The lights went out, then someone—*you*—stabbed me in the neck with an injection thing and knocked me out," she explained, looking very disturbed.

"I didn't stab anyone in a bathroom. I found you crumpled in a heap outside of the cabin in the middle of the night."

"What?!" Her eyes got even bigger, and her skin seemed paler.

She scooted back on the bed as far away from me as she could. So much for not scaring her.

I stepped away and sat in the chair next to the bed, trying to show I wasn't a threat. "How about this? You tell me what you last remember, and then I'll tell you what I remember, and we will figure out how our paths crossed. Does that seem fair?"

She still looked very hesitant but nodded.

"Okay, what is the last thing you remember doing?" I asked, trying to keep my voice gentle. Whatever a human was, she made me think of a small, scared animal—like the kyrrs that hid in the undergrowth of the forest.

"My friends and I got all dressed up to go to the club." At my confused look, she paused. "A club is a place with loud music and dancing and a lot of alcohol, usually."

"So you went to the club for fun?"

"Yes." She seemed relieved that I was following.

"Alright, and what happened at the club?"

"Well, we were all drinking, and I was pretty drunk, and I asked one of my friends to come to the bathroom with me."

"Okay, and you said that is where you were attacked?" I stood to stoke the fire.

"Yes, it all went dark, and everybody disappeared. Then a cold hand grabbed me and that's the last thing I remember."

I took a deep breath. "Alright, my turn. You are on Niflheim, a planet inhabited by orkin. I have never heard of humans before. I have been running for my life for the last several hours. My entire tribe is trying to find me because I refused to marry the jarl's daughter."

I explained to her how I found her, but didn't mention how pretty her little face had been poking out from under her hair.

"Your skin was cold to the touch, and it is freezing up here, so I took you in and did what I could to get you warm. I wasn't sure if you would make it through the night— knowing nothing about how, er, humans function."

She looked at me, incredulous. "So what you're saying is I was dropped here by a UFO."

"I don't know what a UFO is, and until just now, I didn't know there were other places to live outside of Niflheim, but that seems to be true?" I said, voice going up a pitch as if I was asking her for confirmation.

"You don't have a spacecraft?" she asked.

"Nothing that flies."

"And you've never heard of other planets, Earth? Mars?"

"Nope." I was having trouble following what she was saying. I'd never heard most of the words she was using. How did she expect me to know how she got here? She was the one who just appeared out of the sky.

"And you really don't know what a club is?" she asked, giving me a skeptical look.

"Well, it sounds similar to one of our celebrations, but we don't have a place called a *club*," I said, emphasizing the new term.

"So you expect me to believe some other aliens abducted me, and they just decided to leave me here? How do I know you didn't abduct me?"

"Well, for one, do I look like I can fly some sort of sky disk?" I spread my arms wide.

My clothes were made of a mixture of natural fibers and leather. Whatever abducted this human was of a far more advanced species than orkin. She looked me over and then glanced around the room.

"Do you even have electricity here?" she asked, alarmed.

"I don't know what that is." *This is not going well.*

She looked down at her lap and took a couple of steadying breaths. "So, I am not saying I don't believe you. Just let me walk through this. I was abducted by aliens, taken from Earth, and dumped on a planet that not only doesn't have space travel but doesn't even have electricity. Based on this... I have no way home?" She said this very calmly, as if she let herself slip for just a minute, she'd fall apart.

"That seems accurate," I said, unsure if that would make her feel better or worse.

"Okay, and what are your intentions with me?" filled with trepidation.

"What do you mean, my intentions?" Taking my seat back in the chair next to the bed she was still in.

"What do you plan to do with me?"

"Well, so far, I planned to keep you alive through the night. I didn't have a plan beyond that." I shrugged—I really hadn't thought of a long-term plan. *Keep delicate thing alive* was the only thought I had.

"So you saw an alien creature and brought it in, even though you're running for your life?" She looked at me skeptically, pulling the blanket tighter around her bottom half.

"Well, I could see you weren't dressed for the winters up in Niflheim. You're barely wearing any clothes. I couldn't just let you die on my doorstep."

"So there's no end game where you make me your sex slave or lock me in a dungeon?"

I was trying really hard not to be offended while *also* not making her feel like a complete idiot, but it was proving to be challenging.

"No sex slave, no dungeon," I said, voice clipped. "Nurse you back to health and go from there."

I looked again at her pale, skinny shoulder poking out from the blankets with the thin pink tunic strap pushed to the side. She definitely could use a real meal. But seeing her tunic reminded me of the satchel.

"Oh! And you had this with you!" I grabbed the bag from the floor. "Maybe that could explain to us what kind of aliens brought you here?"

She unwrapped herself gingerly, revealing more of the hot pink tunic. I couldn't help but notice how it hugged her curves. It had slid down in the night, and her breasts were almost popping out of it. I averted my gaze as she adjusted herself. As she sat up, she tentatively took the bag from me.

"You found this with me?" she asked as she dumped the contents on the bed. For being such a small bag, it had a lot in it.

I looked at the items from her bag. I didn't recognize any of them. There was a small card with what looked to be the human's face on it. Then it hit me that I'd never even asked her name. I picked up the card and looked at it. There were letters on it, but not in any language I recognized.

"That's my ID. I used it to get in the club," she explained.

"They only let certain humans into the club?"

"You have to be at least twenty-one to drink alcohol, and since clubbing is mostly about drinking and dancing, they only let people who are twenty-one enter."

"And you're twenty-one?" I asked, realizing that based on her size, I couldn't be sure of how old she was.

I hadn't thought of her age until now. She didn't have wrinkles or gray hair like our older orkin, but she seemed to be of age.

"I'm twenty-two. How old are you?"

"I'm twenty-four. I don't know if we measure time in the

same way here, though. How old are you when you are considered of age?"

"Generally eighteen. But you can't drink until you are twenty-one. What about you?"

"We consider sixteen to be of age, but most orkin don't move out of their family home until they take a partner, which ranges."

I looked back at her ID, and she looked sad in the image.

"Why are you sad in your ID?" I asked.

"Oh, the DMV is notorious for taking the worst photos. They don't give you any warning. They snap the photo."

"And it says your name? Can you tell me? I can't read human."

She laughed. "It's not in human. It's in English. We speak English where I am from. My name is Tracy. What's yours?"

"Fenrik. And we don't speak English on Niflheim. We speak Kveoja. How is it that I can understand you? Do you know Kveoja?"

"Nope." She raised her brows, sitting up straighter in the bed. "Are you speaking English?"

"No." I felt like we were making progress, and now we'd reached another hurdle. How were we talking to each other if we didn't even speak the same language?

"Well, that's fucking weird. Maybe the aliens that dumped me here took pity on me and installed a translator in me or something?"

"You think that's possible?" I couldn't bring myself to tell her I didn't understand what "installing a translator" meant, she was already overwhelmed.

"Well, up until about five minutes ago, I didn't believe in aliens, so…" She raised her hands palms up, shrugging as if at a loss. "I guess, I am happy I didn't have some sort of weird alien surgery performed on me."

"Reasonable." I didn't know what else to say, having even fewer answers than she did.

I went back to looking at the contents of her bag. She had several small tubes of what she called "makeup" and a few scraps of paper she said were "receipts." I saw one scrap of paper that looked different and picked it up. It was in a language I recognized, so I held it up.

"Do you recognize this?" I asked.

"No." She shook her head.

I examined the paper. The print was in Kveoja, but it was written in a very odd script. I read it quickly.

Human female. Age: twenty-two Earth years. Category: undesirable. Cause: system compromised by illicit substances.

I had no idea what that meant. *Undesirable? Illicit substances?* I didn't want to say anything to offend her, but this information didn't seem positive. I grimaced at Tracy's expectant face. There was no way around it. I'd have to tell her if we had any hope of figuring it out.

I repeated it to her and asked, "Do you know what that means?"

To my surprise, she laughed.

"They didn't want me because I was drunk!" She snorted, and it was strangely adorable.

"Because you had been drinking alcohol?" I clarified.

"Yep," she said, still laughing. "Actually, I have never been happier that I decided to go out and get wasted. Whatever that creature who abducted me had planned for me has to be worse than your lack of a plan for me, right?"

I tried to think of reasons someone might abduct a human, and I had to admit I couldn't come up with any good ones. I had to agree that my lack of any intent was better than ill intent.

"So, what now?" I asked Tracy.

"I dunno, dude. It's your planet. You tell me."

CHAPTER 4

TRACY

I'd never seen or heard of anything like whatever Fenrik said he was. An orc? He looked like the Incredible Hulk, but less cartoony. And hotter. He was enormous. I could tell even as he sat that he'd tower over me. He had big white tusks jutting from either side of his lower lip and long black hair that gave off a Fabio vibe. I didn't hate it. The sclera of his eyes was light gold, and the irises a nice shade of hazel. From the expression on his face, I gathered he was very concerned. I waited for him to say something. Eventually, the silence got to be too much.

"Let's get this straight. You're on the run from your tribe for refusing to marry the chief's daughter. I've been dumped here by some high-tech aliens for being drunk and I have no way home because you don't even have MTV here. So, we're basically stuck together?" I asked.

"I think that covers everything." His face grew even more concerned.

"You didn't have a plan when you fled from your tribe?" *He must be insane. Who runs with no backup plan?*

"Other than not marrying the chief's daughter, no plan. I can't go to the other tribes on Niflheim because my tribe doesn't have the best reputation, so I fled with nowhere to go. I was backed into a corner."

I couldn't really blame him. I'd also fled, but I at least had the basics of a plan: taking an Amtrak, paying in cash I'd slowly secreted away. But I understood the need to run. All things considered, even here on an alien planet I was in a better situation than I was the year before.

At first, the marriage had been tolerable. Gabe was nice enough to look at, in the boring white kid way most of us in my small town were. His parents were friends with my parents. We all grew up in the same church. We all were the epitome of corn-fed, white America. Our parents put the down payment on a small house a few neighborhoods over from theirs. Gabe worked at his dad's construction company, and I was supposed to be a homemaker.

Only, I didn't want any kids. Or—I didn't want kids with a man I was completely apathetic about. I was on the fence about the whole Christianity thing. The church was insistent that all children were a blessing. I was never outwardly disobedient, but I wasn't going to bring a child into a world I was miserable in. That was a step too far. I was forward-thinking enough to tell Gabe I needed to see the doctor before we were married to make sure everything was in working order. I drove two towns away and went to Planned Parenthood and gave them a fake name. I got a prescription for birth control and a six-month supply.

That worked fine for the first six months. The sex was fine and consensual but incredibly dull. It was when I went to get another six-month supply that things went south. I'd told Gabe that I'd wanted to go to the thrift store two towns over and that was why I needed our shared car, but he seemed skeptical. His skepticism grew when I came home with no clothes. He snatched my purse from me and fished out the birth control. To say he was livid would be an understatement.

I never would have guessed he was capable of violence, but when I packed a small bag that night while he slept, I had a black eye to prove it. I took our car to the Amtrak station, bought a ticket to someplace that sounded warm, and left the car in the parking lot. That's how I ended up working at a shitty diner in San Diego. At least I was free—one of the lucky ones who got out at the first sign of real trouble. From my new home, I could see the ocean every day and come and go as I pleased. When I was in San Diego, there was a small voice in the back of my head that still worried about Gabe finding me. I guess that was one less thing to worry about now.

I looked at Fenrik with my head cocked to the side. "You know, I was on the run, too, when I was abducted."

"From who?"

"My husband."

"What's a husband?"

"Like a partner? Someone you live with? Have babies with?"

"Ah, a mate," he said, like I had any idea what that was. "Why were you running from your mate? Were you fated?"

I didn't have a clue what "fated" meant, but I definitely didn't think I was anything like that to Gabe.

"We don't have *fated* mates where I'm from—just marriage. I never wanted to marry him. My parents picked him for me. It was fine for a while, but when he found out I was taking birth control because I didn't want to have babies with him, he hit me," I explained flatly. It hurt less the faster I got it out.

"He hit you?" Fenrik looked outraged, his fists clenching in anger.

"Yep. Right in my left eye. I packed a bag and left that night."

"Is he still looking for you?"

"I have no idea. I guess it doesn't matter now. He isn't going to find me here." I gave him a sad smile.

"So we were both running from mates we didn't want," he said, brows raised high into his hairline.

"I guess we have that in common, though I'm still trying to understand how mates work for you guys. Like, how do you know you've found the right one?" I scrunched up my face, trying to figure out how that would work.

"Here, it is someone you are bonded to for life—they can be chosen by each other or the fates. Fated mates are called Elska mates. Matching mate marks appear on your back signaling you've found your fated mate. I'd always wanted to find my Elska…" He trailed off and shook himself as if realizing he'd shared more than he'd intended.

Fenrik sat quietly in thought for a long time—so long that I started to feel awkward. "Can I ask what you are thinking?"

Fenrik stood and started pacing around the small space, filling it with nervous energy. "I am trying to decide what to do to help you, but I don't know that my returning to my tribe with you is a good idea." He paused. "Actually, I know it wouldn't be a good idea for *me* to return at this point. Do you want to go to my tribe on your own and see if they will take you in?" He asked.

"Are you crazy? Hell no. If they were ready to kill you over not marrying someone, they don't seem like my kind of people—er, orcs."

"Well, I don't want to return, but I don't want you stuck here with me." He threw up his hands in exasperation and stopped his pacing.

I was putting my foot down. After a life of being forced into things I didn't want to do, I wasn't going to his tribe. It sounded like a very similar life to the one I'd already run from. "I'm not leaving." I crossed my arms over my chest, decision made.

"So you're just going to stay here with me. A stranger that is a different species? How do you know I am not secretly plotting to kill you and eat you?"

He did have a point. I strummed my fingers against my lips. "I think if you were going to murder me, you would have done it by now. It would make the most sense to do it when I was unconscious." Truthfully, he seemed trustworthy up to this point, and it wasn't like I had other options. It was him—or braving the wilderness.

"Do you know how to hunt?"

"That would be a no." But I added pathetically, "I know how to cook, though."

"That should be enough. I can cook basic meals, but if I am doing the hunting, having you help with the cooking would be good. My mother is the tribe's herbalist, so I know all the edible plants. It sounds like we have what it takes to survive while we figure out a long-term plan."

"Well, what now?" I asked.

"I am going to hunt. There's no food in this cabin. Meat is most important. If I can bring down something large, it could feed us for quite a while."

"Can I come with you?" I didn't like the idea of being left alone in the cabin.

"You aren't quite dressed for hunting," he said, giving my neon dress a once over.

"Well, I should do something useful while you are off getting us food." I wasn't going to let this man—er—orc be in charge of me. Been there, done that.

"What do you think you could do that would be helpful to us staying here for a while?"

I wasn't used to being given this kind of agency. I had to think. Though I loathed the idea of domestic chores because it reminded me of my former life, it was probably the most useful thing I could do.

"I could clean the place. If we are going to stay here, we don't need to stay in dust."

"Is that what you want to do?" he asked, looking at me doubtfully.

"No. But it needs doing. I'd like to learn how to forage for food with you so I can take that on, but it can wait until after you've gone hunting. Plus some time alone might be good for me to clear my head. See if I can remember anything else that happened between the bathroom at the club and now. I like that you are giving me a choice of what to do, though.That's new." As I said it out loud, I knew it was exactly what I needed—some time to gather my thoughts. I'd thought fleeing to San Diego was a huge change and now I was apparently on an entirely different planet? My brain was whirring with all the incoming information. Quiet time to process would be good. I nodded to myself, decision made, but I realized Fenrik was still staring at me.

"Your husband ordered you to do things, and you'd do them?"

"Oh, yeah." It took me a minute to remember where the conversation had stopped. "He was the head of the house. I was to be wife and mother."

Fenrik's look was so pitying I wanted to curl up into a ball.

"It's over now. I'm free. Really free. Go, hunt. I'll make this place livable like a good homemaker." I grimaced.

"Promise you won't wander far if you go outside. I don't

want you getting lost." He stood and pulled on his boots. Wow, he was really tall. And muscular.

"I won't travel far. I promise. I need the space to think, and we need food. This is the best plan for the day."

He raised his brows knowingly. "You've already proven you're a runner."

I guess I had just explained to him how I fled from Gabe. "I won't run. You haven't given me any reason to. I also could use the time to decide if I actually believe you aren't going to murder and eat me. You seem pretty normal but also look like the Hulk, so I haven't decided yet."

"The what?" he asked, as he walked around the cabin gathering hunting supplies.

"Never mind, just go hunt. Let me clean house while I sort out that my life just got turned upside down for a second time." I was moments away from telling him to shoo when he headed out the door.

I needed space. Fenrik gave me one last concerned look before shutting the door behind him. Once I was sure he was gone, I wandered around the cabin, gaining my bearings. It hadn't been used in a long time. Everything was covered in a thin layer of dust. I couldn't even begin to imagine what kind of cleaning supplies they had. I looked through the kitchen area and was surprised to find a relatively solid-looking broom. It was a start.

I started in the living area and attacked it with vigor while I thought about what had happened to me in the last… twenty-four hours? I had no way of knowing how long I was unconscious or even what day it was. I checked my armpits. Still pretty freshly shaved, so it couldn't have been more than a day. Did I believe I had been abducted and was now on an alien planet?

I tried repeatedly to remember anything after the club bathroom. And there was nothing. It was blank. I knew very little about Fenrik, but if this was the level of technology this planet had, I knew he didn't abduct me. I was surprised they had running water—no electricity, but running water.

I continued cleaning, finding cloths folded neatly in one of the cupboards that I could use to wipe down the surfaces. The couch was dusty, but I couldn't do much more than try removing the worst part. Then I moved to the bedroom. The bedding was a twisted mess from where I had rolled around at night, trying to stay warm. Not having a washing machine, I decided the best would be to shake it outside to remove the dust and musty smell. I cleaned off a small porch railing, then hung the bedding over it so it could at least get some fresh air. It was cold outside—it felt like early fall in Colorado. My bare feet were freezing on the porch. I hopped back and forth as I hung the blankets out. They would be chilly when I brought them back in, but at least they wouldn't be musty. I worked quickly. I was still in nothing but my borrowed pink dress. I couldn't run even if I wanted to.

I went back inside and realized I'd run out of work to do. The cabin was as clean as I would get it without better cleaning supplies. It was probably mid-afternoon, and I didn't know the last time I had eaten. My stomach was starting to protest, but there wasn't anything I could do but wait for Fenrik to return.

I wandered around the cabin, aimlessly picking up things and putting them down. I tried to find anything else to clean, but there was nothing.

That's fine. I can sit and wait.

I sat on the freshly cleaned couch with my hands in my lap. I was used to being useful, sitting with nothing to do was outside my comfort zone. I managed a whole fifteen minutes of just sitting before I started to spiral. I didn't *know* Fenrik. The rational part of my brain was telling me to just be patient and wait for him to return as he promised he would, but the small voice in the back of my mind saying that he'd just left me in the cabin and moved on was getting louder and louder.

What if he went back to his tribe and never returned for me? What if he was lying and left me here so he could figure out his own problems?

I was more of a burden than anything else. He was at least capable. He could make his way on this planet without worrying about me. Maybe he left me here because it was the easiest option, and he would try to find another tribe to live with or see if his tribe would take him back. I wavered back and forth. He'd only helped me thus far and had given me no reason not to trust him. But then again, ever since I left home, who could I trust?

CHAPTER 5

TRACY

*D*eciding I could at least *look* outside to see if Fenrik was anywhere to be seen, I stepped out of the cabin and down the little porch steps. Looking out into the clearing, I couldn't tell which direction he'd gone. There were footsteps all over the grass from him coming and going. There were only two clear paths out of the clearing. One was probably from where he entered while running from the tribe, which meant the other had to be the one he took to hunt. It was late afternoon and I was shoeless and wearing a barely there dress. I'd been alone in the cabin all day.

What if he never came back?

Choosing the trail that made the most sense based on nothing but intuition, I followed it into the woods. It wasn't bad underfoot, mainly flattened grass. When I reached the trees, it turned into hard-packed dirt. If I stepped gingerly, avoiding the bigger rocks and roots that stuck up, it was manageable. I tried to be as quiet as I could, stepping gingerly along the trail and looking for any sign of Fenrik. It was only a few moments before I reached a fork.

Fuck. Maybe this is a terrible idea.

But what was I going to do? Stay in the cabin and die there? Try to learn what plants were edible through trial and error? None of my worst-case-scenario thinking prepared me for alien abduction. I rolled all of my options around in my head and couldn't come up with any other solution. Standing there with my hands on my hips, trying to pick a path, wasn't going to get me anywhere. I picked the one that looked slightly more worn and followed it. As I walked, I took mental notes of anything I saw that I could use to find my way back: a large oddly shaped boulder, a tree that looked as if it had been split by lightning, and a fallen log covered in moss. As I got further in, the forest got darker, with more of the light blotted out by the giant trees. However, it meant the forest floor was softer on my feet, covered with different mosses. I thought I heard something up ahead and rushed to the noise, hoping to find Fenrik. The ground started to slope down, and the trees thin, and then I saw it.

I skidded to a halt twenty paces away from what looked very much like an Earth bear fishing in the stream. Or at least, that is what I assumed it was doing. It was watching the water very intently and hadn't noticed me. I held back the scream that threatened to erupt and I backed away very slowly, never taking my eyes off of it. When I reached the tree line I felt my foot press down and snap a twig. The noise echoed through the silence. The animal's head swung up and it locked eyes with me. I immediately noticed the differences between it and an Earth bear as it let out a low growl. It had not one, but two rows of pointed teeth, with the front canines extending in a saber-toothed tiger sort of way. Oh, and it had *four* yellow eyes—all of them narrowed on me. *Great.*

I turned on my foot and fled. I didn't bother looking back to see if the bear-thing was following me. I ran flat out for as long as possible, weaving through trees and wincing every time I stepped on a particularly sharp rock. I ran until my lungs burned, and I had a stitch in my side and pushed myself to go even further, blindly panicking. I wasn't going to make it through an alien abduction only to be eaten by a bear.

Eventually, I had to stop, realizing I wasn't on any trail and had no idea where I was. I strained my ears to hear any noise of the bear coming to follow me, but I heard nothing. Suddenly, I felt foolish. I was now even more lost. I tried to take in everything around me, and nothing seemed familiar.

Why would it? Dumb, dumb, dumb Tracy.

I was never going to make it back to the cabin. I didn't even have stupid basic wilderness skills like knowing what side of a tree moss grows on. They didn't teach that in Girl Scouts where I was from. Not that it would matter. So what if moss grew on the north side of the trees if I didn't know if the cabin was north or south of where I was?

All of a sudden it became too much. The adrenaline from my panic at the cabin and then from the bear was slipping out of me. I was exhausted and I slumped down against a tree and started to cry. And not that cute sweet crying that girls do on TV, but big ugly sobs that shook my whole body. I cried for the childhood that I lost to my strict upbringing. I cried for the loveless marriage I'd been forced into. I cried for all the hard work I had put in to build a new life, something that would finally be mine, just to have it all ripped away. Yes, the crappy job at Coco's was a crappy job at Coco's, but it was mine. I had gotten there on my own. I finally had a tiny sliver of freedom and I'd had it all snatched away from me. I sobbed until snot ran out of my nose and I wasn't making any noise. I laid my head down on the forest floor and wished for it to swallow me up as I cried until I had no more tears in me.

I woke to someone gently shaking my shoulder. I opened my eyes to find myself face to face with Fenrik, kneeling in front of me. Concern etched his face as he looked from my tear-streaked face to my dirty and bruised feet.

"What happened?" he asked. "Why did you leave the cabin?"

This was as close as he'd been to me, having given me a wide berth when he first woke me up. Once you got past the startling differences, he was handsome. He had a strong square jaw and full lips that looked soft, with large tusks jutting from either side. His dark brows arched beautifully and were currently creased with concern. Without thinking, I touched his face with just the tips of my fingers. He had the beginnings of a stubbly five-o'clock shadow and was very warm to the touch. I couldn't believe he came looking for me, a stranger—an alien—he'd just met.

"You came looking for me?"

"Of course. You aren't safe in these woods alone. But why did you leave?"

I sighed. "After you were gone all morning, I got this thought in my head that maybe you hadn't gone hunting. That—that—" I faltered.

I didn't want him to think I didn't trust him. Even though he'd given me no reason not to. Now I was ashamed for not trusting that he'd come back. I took a deep breath.

"I thought that maybe I was too much trouble, and you'd gone back to your tribe or gone to join another tribe."

"Why would I leave you behind?" he asked, lips pursed in confusion.

"You only just met me. You don't have any reason to help me," I said, dipping my head in shame.

"I'm helping you because you need help. You've never had a stranger help you just because you needed it?" He seemed almost mad, his massive shoulders bunching up.

I thought of Trish and how she helped me get back on my feet, asking for nothing in return. Sure it wasn't the warmest of support, but it was help nonetheless. All my coworkers saw me struggle to gain footing in a new town where I knew no one and helped me slowly come out of my shell. Maybe it was because Fenrik was male, and males hadn't treated me kindly in the past. I searched his face for any ounce of doubt. He looked determined.

"I know that doesn't excuse me for not giving you a chance, but it is going to take me a while to believe that I can trust you, especially when you're getting nothing in return." I chewed my lower lip.

"But you're willing to try to trust me?" he asked, earnestly.

"If you still want to help me," I mumbled, fidgeting with my hands in my lap. "I wouldn't blame you if you wanted nothing to do with me."

"Hey. We're both kind of stuck. Doesn't it make sense to be stuck with someone else?"

"I suppose." I still felt sorry for myself.

"Alright then, let's head back to the cabin. The sun is going down and I don't want to be stuck out here in the dark."

I stood slowly and winced as I put pressure on my feet. The adrenaline that poured through me as I ran from the bear had made me numb to the damage I'd caused as I ran through the forest. Not only were the bottoms of my feet dirty, but they were covered in cuts and bruises. I had scrapes on my arms and face from where I'd flown by tree branches as fast as I could. It was going to be painfully slow going to get back to the cabin.

I looked at Fenrik and nodded to show him I was ready to go. He headed in the exact opposite direction I would have guessed the cabin to be, so I truly would have been fucked had he not shown up to save me—again.

I hobbled along slowly, pain lancing through me each time I stepped on a rock or a twig. I tried to keep up, but it wasn't long before Fenrik noticed how much I was struggling. He raised his brows at me as I limped forward.

"It's nothing, I'm fine. I just hurt my feet more than I realized running through the forest barefoot." I tried to dismiss his concern and keep walking.

He stopped. "Let me see the bottom of your foot."

"It really is nothing," I said, continuing to walk.

He studied me momentarily as I attempted to pick up my pace and caught the large wince I made when I stepped on another rock.

"Feet. Now." He pointed at the ground.

Feeling incredibly embarrassed, I sat down on the ground so he could see the bottoms of my feet. I grimaced as he scrutinized them, noting all the dried blood and even some fresh blood from where I'd reopened cuts as we walked. Fenrik furrowed his brow and stood.

"I'm going to carry you," he stated, not asked.

"No, no. I don't want you to carry me. I can walk." I stood and brushed myself off. It was one thing to start to trust Fenrik, but I didn't know if I could bear to have to wrap my body around his in the way necessary for me to be carried. I wasn't ready to be touched by a man like that. Not after Gabe. Not that I ever put up a fight with him, but it wasn't ever really my choice. Just doing my wifely duties.

"I don't think I can handle you touching me," I said, chewing on my lower lip.

"Because of your mate?" He caught on immediately.

"Yeah, I really don't like being touched unless I initiate it. It makes my skin crawl."

"Your skin does what?" he asked, looking alarmed.

"Ha, it's slang. It means it makes me feel really uncomfortable." I laughed and wondered what other Americanisms Fenrik had never heard.

But he continued to look very serious. "We need to get home and get home now. What if I wrap you in my cloak so my skin isn't actually touching yours?"

I had already caused this poor orc so many problems, and here he was, trying to work with me instead of just throwing up his hands and leaving me to die in the wilderness. I felt terrible.

"Okay, you can carry me in your cloak. Will you be warm enough though?" I asked as the sun continued to sink in the sky.

"Já, as long as we get on our way. I don't want to get caught out here when the predators start to come out for the night." He unhooked his cloak and handed it to me.

I wrapped it around me like a giant towel. Fenrik approached me slowly and scooped me up, carefully placing one hand on my back and the other under my knees, as if he could tell these were the safest places to touch. I clutched my arms to my chest, trying to settle.

"Is this okay?" he asked, as he pulled me against his body, preparing to walk.

I nodded. He was very tall and very warm. But I felt okay. I felt safe.

"Then let's be off. You managed to cover a great distance with your tiny injured feet." He started at a brisk pace, jostling me so I had to lean into his chest.

I felt something shift. Something small and fragile, but a tiny flame inside me dared to hope that I might let my walls down with this giant, kind-eyed orc.

CHAPTER 6

FENRIK

I tried not to stare down at Tracy while I hurried back to the cabin. She sat with her arms crossed in front of her, staring off into the distance. I wanted to be frustrated that she'd wandered off, but I couldn't be. She was right. She had no reason to believe I'd return. Tracy didn't know I had spent most of the afternoon hunting. She was gone when I returned to the cabin with the animal I'd managed to bring down. The cabin was pristine—but no Tracy. At first I panicked, but there were no signs of a struggle. Tracy seemed like the type that would put up a fight.

I left my kill on the back porch and spent the rest of the afternoon and into the early evening looking for her. Injured and asleep on the forest floor was not how I expected to find her. It was going to be a long night. I still had to butcher the animal and cook it. Neither of us had eaten in more than a day now.

After some time, Tracy shifted in my arms, and I realized

she'd fallen asleep and was leaning into my chest instead of sitting stiffly as she had when she was awake. She reminded me of a kyrr, small and timid. They often hid in the forest's undergrowth and were rarely seen by orkin. I pulled Tracy closer to me as she slept, wanting to protect her from not only from our planet's predators and harsh weather but also from the pain she'd already endured. She was right. I could have just left, but something about her called out to me, telling me to stay with her. I sighed, knowing as well as she did that we had no long-term plan, but we had to just focus on living through each day for the time being. For today, that meant food—and hopefully getting clean.

I reached the clearing as the sun slid behind the mountains, leaving us in the blue twilight of early evening. Tracy was quietly snoring into my chest and had turned her body even closer to me as if trying to absorb my warmth.

I carried her into the cabin, careful to keep my movements gentle as I laid her on the couch. She stirred slightly but didn't wake, her features softening even more in the warm glow of the fading light. I paused for a moment, just watching her. The way her chest rose and fell with each breath, the delicate curve of her lips—it was mesmerizing. My body started to warm in all sorts of ways, and I knew I needed to stop staring. No matter how drawn I found myself to her, I shouldn't be ogling a sleeping human.

I focused on starting a fire but stole glances at her as I moved about the small space. The cabin felt intimate, the rough wood walls enclosing us in a cozy embrace. I gathered kindling and logs from the nearby stack, my thoughts lingering on her. She was so different from me—so fragile yet fierce in her own right. It struck me how much strength it took her to be out here, facing the unknown.

As I crouched by the hearth, striking flint against stone, I caught sight of her again. Her hair fanned out on the couch, catching the last bits of sunlight filtering through the window, making the yellow of her waves appear more golden. I could still see the faint traces of worry on her face from earlier, but now, in deep sleep, she looked serene. This made me fiercely desire to protect her, to keep the darkness of my world and her past at bay.

The fire caught, crackling to life, casting warm shadows across the cabin. I added more wood, feeling the heat spread through the air. As I turned back to her, I noticed how she instinctively curled into herself, as if seeking warmth even in her dreams. A smile tugged at my lips—again, she reminded me of the kyrr—small, hidden away, yet filled with an undeniable spirit. I moved closer, settling onto the edge of the couch, wanting to be near her. Tonight, I would keep her safe and feed her.

The fire popped, pulling me out of my wandering thoughts and reminding me there was much more to be done. I needed to butcher the animal before we lost all the light. I pulled a blanket over Tracy before heading out to the back porch. I would work quickly so she wouldn't wake up and worry that I left her again.

Tracy

I was snuggled comfortably in my warm bed, a soft blanket cocooning me. Faint sounds of movement pulled me from my peaceful state, and I blinked, only to realize that I was most definitely not in my bedroom in San Diego. Panic surged through me before the memories rushed back. This was a cabin on an alien planet. I was here with Fenrik, the orc who was taking a serious risk in providing me a place to stay. He was committed to seeing me through this alive, and I was almost ready to believe him. *Breathe in, breathe out.*

Sitting up, I ran my fingers through my hair, the familiar gesture grounding me. My borrowed pink dress I was wearing still felt foreign, and I longed for something more practical, especially considering the cold. I wrapped the blanket tighter around myself, wishing for a moment that I could shake off the remnants of my old life.

Time slipped away as I sat in front of the fire, reveling in the warmth and the rare stillness that enveloped me. Back home, I had never had the luxury to rest—with Gabe, there was always something expected of me—cleaning, cooking, maintaining the façade of our perfect life. But here, in this cabin, I could breathe.

Eventually, though, it was clear that Fenrik wasn't in the cabin, and unease began to creep in again. I stood up, wincing slightly at the pain in my feet, and made my way to the window facing the back porch. When I peeked outside, I gasped at the sight before me.

Fenrik was stripped to the waist, and the moonlight cast a silvery glow over his bulging muscles as he focused intently on butchering an animal. It looked a little bit like a goat, with shaggy fur and short stubby antlers, but it had long slender legs like a deer. Whatever it was, I hope it tasted good.

I continued to watch as Frenrik's broad shoulders and powerful arms moved with precision, and his muscles rippled as he worked. Something unexpected fluttered in my chest, watching him work. *Was I ogling an orc?*

The last time I had been *intimate* with a man, I shut my eyes and let Gabe do the work. No feelings or desire attached. It was absurd to be thinking lusty thoughts about a man I barely knew. I tried to dismiss the warmth I felt pooling in my belly. Yet, here I was, captivated by how the moonlight danced across his skin, highlighting the strength in every movement. There was something primal about him, something that spoke to the very core of my being. He was so different from Gabe, so raw and unapologetic, and I found myself drawn to him. I couldn't help it. Fenrik had protected me and cared for me when no one else had. In a world so foreign, he was a steadfast presence, and the more I watched him, the more I felt that maybe, just maybe, I could allow myself to feel something for him.

He finished cutting the meat into manageable pieces and paused for a moment, as if sensing my gaze. His eyes lifted and met mine through the window, and a rush of warmth flooded my cheeks, embarrassed to be caught watching him. As he tentatively smiled, I smiled back.

I wobbled back to the couch, still tired, the pain in my feet lancing through me with each gentle step I took. Soon Fenrik returned inside, giving me another brief smile before turning to the counter to deposit the meat. My stomach grumbled at the thought of food, and I briefly wondered how long it had been since the last time I had eaten. Fenrik took quite a bit of time at the sink, washing up to his elbows and then opening and looking through the cupboards. I tried to sit quietly and not pester him with questions. After what seemed an age, he returned to me on the couch, not with food as I expected.

"I know you are hungry, but we must tend to your feet first. They won't heal in their current state." He set a bowl of steaming water and strips of cloth on the table. Then, he pulled a small glass jar out of his pocket and placed it on the table along with the other supplies. "I found some healing ointment and healing essentials in the kitchen. I need your feet."

"Oh n-no, it's—it's o-okay," I stuttered. "I am sure they'll be fine." I blushed furiously. I didn't need this hulking orc touching my dirty and bloodied feet. It seemed too... intimate.

"Tracy." His gravelly voice came out stern. "They won't

heal unless properly cleaned and bandaged, and you can't do that on your own. Again, I need your feet."

The tone of his voice, while not harsh, left no room for argument. I lifted my feet, unsure of where he wanted me to place them, and was surprised when he gently took my ankles and guided my feet into his lap. His hands were huge and calloused but unexpectedly gentle as he inspected each foot. Given my angle, I couldn't see most of what he was looking at, but if the dirt and dried blood streaked across the top of my feet were any indicator, I had to guess it was bad.

He dipped a cloth into the steaming water and paused before starting. "This is likely going to hurt, but we can't have your feet getting infected." He looked almost mournful that he was going to have to cause me pain.

I nodded, bracing myself. As Fenrik began to clean my feet, I couldn't help but wince. The warm water stung as it made contact with my raw skin, and I bit my lip to keep from crying out.

"I'm sorry," Fenrik murmured, his brow furrowed in concentration. "I'll try to be as gentle as I can."

Despite the discomfort, I was mesmerized by how he tended to my wounds. His large hands moved with surprising delicacy, supporting my ankle with one while the other worked methodically to clean away the dirt and blood. The cloth he used was soft against my skin, and I could feel the warmth of his fingers through the fabric.

"You're doing well," he said, glancing up at me reassuringly. "The worst of it is almost over."

I felt a flutter in my chest at his words, warmth spreading through me that had nothing to do with the water. As Fenrik continued his ministrations, I found myself studying him more closely. The narrowed look of concentration in his eyes, the way his tusks peeked out slightly when he frowned, the gentle way his calloused thumbs brushed against my skin as he worked—all of it captivated me. The pain in my feet began to fade into the background as I became lost in the rhythm of his movements.

The moon rose in the sky, and the fire crackled as he worked silently, creating an almost dreamlike atmosphere.

He gently started spreading the ointment across the ball of my foot, and I sighed in relief. I felt my body relax as he spread it all over the bottom of each foot. It was almost as if I could feel it starting to heal my feet. I held my breath as he meticulously covered each toe in the salve. It tickled, but I was determined to stay still for him.

As if he felt me tense, his eyes met mine. "Does it hurt?"

"No, no." I placed my hand over my mouth, trying to stop the giggle bubbling up in my stomach from escaping to no avail. Fenrik dropped his brows in confusion. "Sorry! It tickles!"

Fenrik's face shifted from concerned to mischievous. "Oh, you mean this tickles?" He dragged a feather-light touch across the arch of my foot, causing me to squirm.

"Yes!" Full-blown laughter came out of me with a gasp. "Stop, stop! This surely can't be good for my *healing*."

With a small grin still lingering, he started slowly wrapping my feet in the strips of cloth, neatly bandaging each foot. He finished but didn't take his warm hands off my ankles, still studying his handiwork.

"Um… are you planning on keeping my feet?" I joked.

I was surprised to see him blush.

"No, no," he said, gently taking them from his lap and placing them on the couch. "They are just so small and delicate—like the rest of you." He raised his eyes to meet mine. "I was so worried when you disappeared."

My cheeks began to feel warm as he gazed at me, his words suspended in silence. As if realizing what was happening, he cleared his throat and stood.

"You should stay off of them as much as possible while they are healing, so I will cook us some dinner."

As he headed to the kitchen, I called out, "So I am just supposed to sit here like a bump on a log?"

"Like a… *what?*"

With his face scrunched up in confusion, I couldn't help but laugh again. American slang clearly didn't translate.

"Like a lazy person," I explained.

He looked affronted. "You're not lazy! You're injured." He returned to preparing something for us to eat, giving me no further room to argue.

CHAPTER 7

FENRIK

I made a quick work of cutting and skewering the meat. I found some basic seasonings in the cupboard and brought the meat to the low table in front of the fire where Tracy sat, feet out in front of her as I had instructed. I hooked the skewers in the notches over the fire made for just that purpose. As long as I rotated the meat often, it would be done quickly.

As I sat next to her on the couch, I caught Tracy looking at me with her mouth hanging open.

"You can, like, actually cook?" She seemed genuinely puzzled.

"I can cook. Do you know how to cook?" I asked, confused by her question.

"Yes, yes. But back home, it was always the wife's duty to cook. My husband could barely handle boiling water."

"He seems kind of useless," I responded. To my delight, she laughed, a big, full, beautiful laugh, before settling into silence while I rotated the meat as it cooked. Soon it was done, and I slipped it off the skewers and onto some plates I found, along with basic cutlery.

"I guess he was kind of useless in some ways," Tracy said eventually, returning to our earlier topic. Smiling, she popped a piece of the meat into her mouth.

She groaned through her mouthful. "This is delicious. How did you do this without any seasoning?"

"I found some basic herbs and spices in the kitchen. Most of them are old, but there was enough to give the meat at least a bit of flavor." I tried not to show how pleased I was that she liked my cooking. It really was just sticks of meat. I didn't have a lot to work with out here. "Maybe we can go foraging for more herbs and other options once your feet heal."

"I'd like that," she said, taking another bite.

Considering the enthusiasm with which she was attacking her food, I decided I should also eat. The meat was good, if a little bland. I could do better, and now that I saw how much she appreciated it, it would become my mission to make her delicious things. It didn't sound like she'd ever had someone cook for her. We ate in companionable silence for a while, and I was surprised but pleased to see she cleared her plate.

"Do you want more?" I asked. I had only given her one skewer of meat.

"No, no, I am completely full. Thank you. I didn't realize how hungry I was. I have been running on adrenaline all day, and now I am full and exhausted," she said, looking into the crackling fire.

"Do you want to clean up before you go to sleep? I can make you a bath with one of the large metal tubs. You will just have to take care with your feet."

"Is there any other way to get clean here?" she asked,

eying the tubs stacked in the kitchen's corner. They were mainly used for washing clothes when the stream was frozen over, but she was small enough that it would work for her to bathe in.

"Unfortunately, this cabin is far from any of our hot springs. There is a stream, but it would be ice cold," I explained, assessing her reaction.

"I'd really like to get all of me clean." She said, frowned at her dirty dress, then hesitantly looking at me.

"Well, after all the effort you've gone to get the bedding aired out and clean, you don't want to sleep in it dirty. I don't mind. I insist."

"Do you think there are any extra clothes here?" Tracy tugged her tight dress down as if remembering just how exposed she really was. "I'd hate to put my dirty dress back on."

I could tell she was uncomfortable asking for even more help but *more* uncomfortable being so dirty.

"Let me go look." I stood and headed to the bedroom.

I rummaged through the closet and small dresser and found suitable clothing for Tracy, if not quite large, and, thankfully, towels.

When I returned, Tracy was looking into the flickering fire. I held up what I'd found, and she looked so grateful for some used clothes and a towel that it made my heart clench.

"How are you going to get the giant bucket out of the fire?" she asked, looking confused from the bucket to me.

"With my arms?" I used two of the rags I found—so as not to burn my hands—and lifted the giant bucket off the hook in the fire and set it down next to it. Tracy's eyes got very large.

"You are really strong," she whispered in awe.

"I'm just a lot bigger than you. And trained to hunt down animals much larger than me," I added, almost as an afterthought. "Let me build up the fire in the bedroom while you bathe so you can have some privacy."

I took some logs from the shrinking pile beside the fireplace and headed into the bedroom. I would have to cut more wood in the morning. I got the fire in the bedroom to a roaring flame and returned to the living room. Tracy would need more time, so I headed out the second door of the small bedroom to the porch to finish butchering the animal. I cut off all the usable meat and set aside the skins to cure it into leather. I hadn't done any leatherwork since my training as a hunter, but I thought of all we might need out here in the cabin, and we would definitely make use of it.

I cleaned the entire porch and arranged some meat for drying and the rest for eating over the next few days. The meat would stay cold in the small cellar under the porch. While waiting, I wondered what else I could do when I saw Tracy approach the sink through the kitchen window.

I headed inside to find Tracy, freshly clean, with wet hair, attempting to do dishes.

"Tracy. You are on your feet," I said sternly, causing her to yelp in surprise. "I know you don't like relying on anyone and you're still unsure about me, but the only way your feet are going to heal is if you stop trying to use them. Do you want me to carry you to the bedroom?"

She opened her mouth to protest, then shut it. In her oversized tunic and leggings, she looked even smaller, but at least she was clean. She set the dishes in the sink and shuffled toward the bedroom, with me close behind her. She climbed into the bed, pulling the covers around her. Once she was settled, I turned to leave so she could sleep.

"Fenrik, will you stay?" she asked quietly. Seeing the surprised look on my face, she continued. "Will you just sit with me until I fall asleep? I don't want to be alone."

I returned to her and sank into the chair beside the bed. "I'll stay for as long as you'd like."

"Thank you," she whispered, tucking her hand under her pillow, "for everything. For today and last night. I'd probably be dead if you hadn't found me." Her big blue eyes started to fill with tears. "And I was stupid enough to go and make it even harder to keep me alive."

"No, no. You did what was reasonable, given everything that has happened to you. I am not going to let you blame yourself for all of this. I won't leave you again without telling you how long I think I will be gone, and I will always return. Once you are healed, you can even come with me. Maybe we'll make a hunter out of you."

Tracy laughed, wiping the tears from her eyes. I loved how easy it was to get her to laugh—the sound lit up the room.

"I sincerely doubt I would be any use at hunting, but I could probably forage?"

"Mm, yes. We could definitely go foraging." I paused. "Once you are asleep, I am going to bathe in the stream. I won't be gone long, and it is very close to the cabin."

Concern flicked across Tracy's face. "Won't the stream be cold? Why can't you use the tub I used?"

"Yes, it will be cold, but I have done it before. And I am quite a bit larger than you." I spread my arms so she could see my large frame. "I wouldn't even be able to fit half of me in that tub."

Tracy let out another small giggle as her eyelids drooped. "I suppose that's true," she said sleepily.

"I won't be gone long, I promise."

I hated to leave her again, but the stream was close, and I was filthy. Tracy nodded and closed her eyes. It was mere moments before her breathing slowed, and I could tell she'd drifted off to sleep. I quietly left the room, pulling the door shut behind me. Then I grabbed soap and towels from the small washroom and headed down to the stream.

It was close enough to the cabin that if anything were to happen, I could hear Tracy scream, but I quickly removed my clothes, anyway. I shuddered as I stepped into the water—even with my thick skin, the cold cut through me like a knife. I stepped in up to my waist, attempting to ignore the cold. As I scrubbed away the grime, my thoughts wandered back to Tracy. I remembered her delicate features, soft laughter, and how her eyes sparkled when she smiled. I started to think of the smooth curve of her bare thighs and the way her tiny tunic hugged her ass, but I banished the thoughts from my mind. Things between us were too fragile—too raw for me to be thinking of her that way.

Shivering when I stepped out of the stream, I realized I had forgotten to bring a change of clothes. I wrapped myself in a towel and quickly returned to the cabin. I found some loose linen pants tucked into the corner of the dresser and made the couch into a bed. The fire crackled merrily, and my mind drifted to Tracy again as I let the warmth lull me to sleep. What was this tiny woman doing to my mind?

CHAPTER 8

TRACY

The next several days drifted into a pattern with Fenrik hunting and gathering what he could from the surrounding forest while I tried deep cleaning the cabin. Whenever Fenrik was in the cabin, he would insist I sit and rest my feet so they would heal. He wouldn't let me cook or do any house chores while he was home, so I tried to do as much as I could secretly when he hunted. I had a feeling he knew, though, since every time he returned, each part of the cabin was a little bit cleaner. Finally, after over a week, I declared myself healed enough to leave the cabin and start helping more.

I was sitting on the couch while he cooked dinner in the kitchen when I told him that was my last day staying cooped up.

"Your feet need to heal," he said, not even looking up from the meat he was dicing.

"They are healed! I promise!"

They didn't hurt anymore and the deep cuts were now healed over nicely. I had them propped up on the table in front of the fire, still bandaged, with socks on. Fenrik washed off his hands and headed over to me. I was in my pink dress because all our other clothes were hanging to dry. I bit my lip as he walked toward me.

He'd been careful about touching me since he knew it was something I was nervous about, but it didn't mean I hadn't been... *admiring him* over the last several days. I'd noticed how often he watched me when he thought I wasn't looking over the last week. It made me wonder if he was feeling the same growing attraction I was feeling for him. *Does he want to touch me?* I thought about the idea of touching him and I felt flushed. It was tempting to imagine touching him in return, but also terrifying.

Fenrik sat down next to my feet. "May I?"

I scrunched my nose in embarrassment but was okay with his touch. It wasn't as if he hadn't seen my feet before. "If you must."

He took one foot in his hand, gingerly pulled down the sock, and removed it. As before, his fingers were rough and calloused and so, so warm. He moved to unwrap the strips of cloth I'd been using as bandages.

"Does this hurt?" He gently removed the fabric from the bottom of one foot.

"Nope." He eyed me suspiciously as if I might be lying. "I promise, look! They are nothing more than healed scratches at this point."

Fenrik traced a rough fingertip along one of my larger scratches. I broke out in goosebumps and felt my breath catch in my throat. Fenrik didn't seem to notice, moving to inspect my other foot. I held my breath as his hands worked over my feet, inspecting every part of them for injury. I felt a somewhat unfamiliar warmth pool in between my legs. It had happened when I watched him butcher our meal our first night and had now happened several times. Generally, when he was shirtless. I was no virgin. I had put two and two together. I was just so afraid of being the first one to say anything. Maybe I was misreading those furtive looks he was giving me.

But here he was, still touching my feet, though they were clearly healed enough for me to leave the confines of the cabin and help with the daily chores. He finished his inspection, gave a small *hmpf* and stood. He looked me over once more before he headed to the back door and opened it wordlessly. He stepped outside but left the door open. He was gone just long enough for me to start to wonder what he was doing when he returned carrying something. Sitting back down on the table beside my feet, he showed me what he was carrying.

A small pair of leather boots.

"Where did you get those?" I gasped.

"I made them." He looked at me nervously. "Do you like them?"

"You made them?!" I snatched them from his hands and held them up to the light so I could examine the detail.

While they were definitely handmade, the stitching was tiny and impressive. It must have taken him hours to do this.

"When did you—"

He cut me off. "While you slept at night. I started them with the leather from the animal I caught on my first hunt," he said, awaiting some judgment.

"I think they're amazing," I said in a low voice. "How did you know my size?"

"Really?" He looked as if he couldn't believe his ears and flushed. "I may have taken a quick measurement the last time I rebandaged you."

I took one and pulled it on. It fit perfectly. I slipped on the other one and then looked down at my feet, grinning like an idiot. I'd never been more happy for a pair of shoes in my life. Without thinking, I pulled Fenrik in for a hug. We hadn't touched like this since he carried me back from my venture out into the woods. And even then, it wasn't an embrace. Fenrik froze momentarily, as if unsure what to do, before wrapping his arms around my waist and pulling me toward him. I let out a tiny squeak but continued to hug him. This felt good. It felt right. And he smelled good—really good.

Now that I had shoes, Fenrik was willing to let me come hunt and forage with him. He had strict rules about when I could tag along, but he wasn't controlling in the way Gabe was. I knew he just wanted to keep me safe.

It was as if that hug had broken some unspoken barrier, and now Fenrik was constantly looking for excuses to touch me in small ways. He'd touch my hands and linger when showing me how to set a trap, or he'd place his palm on the small of my back if we walked up a particularly steep path looking for berries or mushrooms. I wanted to lean into it every time he did it, but I was so nervous. I was quite sure I wanted to touch him more, but I'd never done whatever this was this before. Dating? Having feelings for someone? *What if I was misreading everything?*

One night, I was sitting on the couch next to the fire, sewing up a tear in one of Fenrik's tunics, trying not to bring it to my nose and sniff it. *Don't be a fucking weirdo, Tracy.* Fenrik sat down next to me with a small knife and a piece of wood in his hand. He had been whittling away at something in the evenings but wouldn't tell me what it was. I was guessing it was some surprise for me. As he sat, I looked up and smiled at him, a stray hair falling in front of my eyes. He reached out and tucked it behind my ear. Unconsciously, I leaned into the touch. Fenrik's warm palm was cupping my cheek, and I felt electrified.

"Fenrik?" The unspoken question of what we were doing hung in the air.

Fenrik dropped his whittling on the table and brought his other hand to trace a calloused finger along my jaw.

"Tracy?" he asked, voice husky.

"If you want to touch me more, that would be okay," I whispered, not wanting to ruin the moment.

Fenrik slipped his hand from my cheek to my neck without skipping a beat. He leaned in and nuzzled into my hair, breathing deeply.

"You smell… wonderous," he breathed into my hair.

"Well, you smell pretty damn good, yourself."

I pulled back to look at him. His eyes were hooded with want. *Can I? Should I?*

My body was already deciding for me. I leaned in and pressed my lips against his. At first, they were firm and unyielding, as if he didn't know what to expect. Then, as I nibbled along his lower lip, he opened for me so that I could snake my tongue across his. I felt his breath catch as I stroked my tongue across his—maybe orcs didn't kiss?

"Is this… new for you?" I pulled back.

"Um, I have never done it before, but I would very much like to continue," Fenrik responded.

Okay. So, orcs don't kiss. That could be taught. Right?

I pressed my lips against his firmly, my tongue seeking his. He opened his mouth for me, letting my tongue in. The textured feel of it was new to me, and I wanted more. Our tongues sparred back and forth as he held me close to him, ratcheting up my want. I didn't know what to expect, but I wanted *more*.

Fenrik

What was this tangled dance we were engaged in? Tracy took me by surprise when brushed her soft lips against mine, and now our tongues were tangled up in some erotic movement. I groaned at the soft slide of her tongue against mine, ready to accept what she was offering. She slid her fingers into my hair, holding me close to her as she continued to devour me. Tracy had always seemed so timid and unsure; it was as if whatever we were doing unlocked another side of her. I pulled back.

"What is this?" I asked.

"Kissing, or making out. Very common for humans," she said before pulling me in for another *kiss*.

I wrapped an arm around her waist, pressing us closer together. Oh, how I had wanted this. I didn't know it was an option. Tracy pulled her lips from mine and slowly pressed them down my neck. I didn't know if this still qualified as kissing, but it felt amazing. I ran my fingers through her hair and groaned at the feeling of her lips on my skin. Finally, she kissed her way back up to my mouth, where our tongues continued to tangle together. I wanted to pull her into my lap, but I didn't want to do anything she wasn't ready for. And if I pulled her onto me, she would be very aware of the bulge growing in my pants. Eventually, she broke away and looked at me, eyes hooded and lips swollen.

"I—I want to do more, but I don't know if we should," she said apologetically.

I knew her past. The last thing I wanted to do was pressure her into something she wasn't ready for, no matter how loud my cock was protesting in my pants. Yet, I couldn't deny the ache I felt at her pulling away.

"Okay, do you want to stop now?" I dragged a thumb across her jaw.

"No, but we should," she said sadly and kissed me again. "I don't want to mess this up by going too fast."

She looked disappointed but resolute as she stood and headed for the bedroom.

"Goodnight." She looked at me as if I would be going to sleep any time soon.

She slipped into the bedroom and shut the door, leaving me with a raging hard-on and a little carved jewelry dish I was whittling for her. I wanted to follow her and continue so badly, but more than anything I didn't want to make her uncomfortable. Yet, looking down at the tent in my pants I had to do something to find release.

My cock was so hard it ached, so I slipped out the back door and headed to the stream. I wasn't going to get in, but I would at least be far enough that Tracy wouldn't hear me. I headed about twenty yards from the cabin and positioned myself behind a tree before unlacing my pants and freeing my swollen cock. I was rock hard and already leaking at the tip. Whatever this *kissing* business was, it was doing nothing for my restraint. I thought of the soft slide of Tracy's tongue as I roughly tugged up and down my cock. I didn't know why orkin didn't kiss, but it was an opportunity they were missing out on. I placed my palm against one of the trees as I stroked myself. I thought of Tracy's lips, of her tiny pert breasts, of her rounded ass. She'd opened the floodgates. I no longer felt guilty for the desire I felt for her. She clearly felt it, too.

I came so hard my vision swam as I pictured pulling Tracy into my lap. The arc of my cum was impressive as I continued to slam my hips into my fist. I'd go as slow as Tracy wanted, but even so, I imagined many nights out here in the woods.

CHAPTER 9

TRACY

J was all wound up and had no way to release. I had tried *touching* myself before, even though my youth group leader expressly forbade it. But I was always so nervous that nothing came of it. I closed the bedroom door on Fenrik, torn. I wanted more, but I knew I was worried about the judgment—the backlash. I'd been ready to have sex with my first boyfriend at fifteen, but the idea that I might lose my entire church community stopped me from going forward with it.

Physically, I was ready to ride Fenrik until I couldn't see straight, but mentally, I was worried about the judgment that would fall upon me. I needed to take this slow with him—my brain was telling me that jumping him right now was not okay, even if it was exactly what I wanted to do. I was in bed with my head buzzing with excited thoughts of seeing Fenrik naked, eyes focused solely on me. I wanted... *something.*

I pulled my pants off and lay in just my tunic. The fire crackled merrily in my room because Fenrik always ensured it was well-stocked. I thought briefly of him sleeping on the couch. I wanted to invite him in and curl up with him in the soft bed. He was so warm. The idea of sleeping with him was wonderful and also a bit terrifying. What would others think of me? Then again, for the foreseeable future, there were no others. I knew he'd take care of me every step of the way, but the idea of judgment from church elders—and youth members—was never far from my head.

I parted my bare legs, sliding my fingers down into my curls. There was no one here watching me or judging me. My youth leader wasn't there, and my youth group was gone. I could explore. I slid my finger up and down each lip, feeling how swollen and warm they were. My mind wasn't ready for Fenrik, but my body definitely was. On top of the church indoctrination, I'd always shared a room with my younger sister. Self-exploration was strictly off-limits.

I shifted from stroking my lower lips to gently stroking my clit. I sighed. This was always the problem. I had never figured out how much pressure was enough, but not too much. It was so sensitive that direct contact made me seize up. I tried circling the edges of it slowly while thinking about Fenrik's tusked mouth. If they didn't kiss, did they do oral? I'd given blow jobs before and I enjoyed the *idea* of them— watching a man come undone with just my hands and my mouth. I thought about what it might be like to suck Fenrik's cock and felt myself grow wetter. Watching that giant masculine orc lose control from my touch ratcheted up my desire. Thinking about sucking his cock while slowly circling my clit had me panting and twisting, my body reaching for something that still felt elusive.

I circled around my clit some more, finding myself holding my breath at the sensation that spread out from my core. I imagined Fenrik's cock stuffing me full. I dipped two fingers inside my wet channel while continuing to use my thumb on my clit. I tried pumping my fingers up and down, but they didn't fill me the way a cock would—the way his cock would. I upped the pressure on my clit and bit down on a moan. I didn't want him to know what I was doing. Finally reaching the right rhythm with my fingers and my thumb, I felt an orgasm starting to build. It was a small wisp of a thing. I pulsed in and out rapidly while stroking my clit with my thumb and finally came with a small whimper, with the image of Fenrik's cock at the front of my mind. Yes, I had come before—yet it was rare. But I wanted to come around Fenrik's cock, not my own hand.

Tears pricked at my eyes as the heady wonder of orgasming eviscerated the feelings of guilt and shame I carried from my life on Earth. Thinking of Fenrik while clamping down on my fingers had made me come in a way I never had before.

I rubbed my eyes with the heels of my palms, taking a few steadying breaths. I was here now. The past was gone. More gone than I ever expected it to be. I had been taking tiny steps toward this moment since I met Fenrik, but I finally felt free of the past. I wanted to be with Fenrik and there was nothing standing in my way.

The next morning, I dressed and left the bedroom, unsure what to expect. Fenrik and I had crossed some invisible line the night before and I didn't know what that would mean. He was up and dressed, making breakfast. I walked up to him at the stove.

"Hi," I said, unsure of the greeting I would receive.

"Hi" He bent and brushed a kiss across my lips. Chaste, but a kiss nonetheless.

So what were we now? Dating? A couple? My brain ping-ponged back and forth. I didn't know how any of this worked. I was also theoretically still married to Gabe, but he was on another friggin' planet.

Fenrik continued to cook breakfast—meat and sauteed alien mushrooms—so I set the table. Surely Fenrik would want more—I wanted more. *Right now.* It was just a question of how fast that more would come. Fenrik brought breakfast to the table and sat down with me.

"So, what are your plans for the day?" I asked.

"Well, we could use more meat, so I was thinking of going on a hunt." He looked at me, clearly wishing he could stay with me for the morning—but we did need more meat. The stores had maybe two strips of dried meat left, which was half a meal to me or basically not even a snack to Fenrik.

"I could clean up the cabin and maybe bathe in the stream?"

I knew he was nervous about me going out on my own, but I needed to get clean, and I didn't want him to have to spend time making me another bath.

"Are you sure you will be warm enough?" he asked, holding his fork aloft.

"We have plenty of towels, and hunting needs to happen more than bathing does," I assured him.

"Okay, don't stray farther than the steam?"

"I won't." For some reason, his protectiveness of me didn't grate against me the way Gabe's did.

We finished breakfast, and Fenrik headed off to hunt, but not before kissing me deeply at the door. I had the entire day to mull over what this new step meant. I bathed in the stream, cleaned the cabin, and aired out the bedding. *Why did I air out the bedding? What was I expecting?*

Fenrik returned midafternoon with three kills. He'd had a very successful hunt. He took them to the back porch to butcher while I got the kitchen ready for whatever he decided we'd have for dinner. As he continued to work on his kills I considered that he'd likely want to bathe after butchering multiple animals, so I pulled out the tub he'd used for me and filled it with water before dragging it in front of the fire. It was far too heavy and large for me to place inside the fire, but I hoped putting it on the hearth would warm the water somewhat. I knew it was too small for him, but it had to be better than the stream. I prepared some vegetables we'd foraged while he butchered outside, wishing for him to return.

Finally, he arrived with two steaks in hand. I started heating the worn skillet and indicated toward the bath I'd set up for him. He looked surprised.

"You shouldn't be constantly bathing in the cold. I'll cook the dinner while you get clean," I explained, taking the steaks from him.

I was getting better at finding my way around the kitchen. I cooked all of our meals back home, but things like Rice-A-Roni and Shake 'n Bake. Not, *here's a slab of meat, turn it into something edible.* I took the steaks to the counter and set about making skewers of vegetables and meat that could be cooked over the fire. I had seen Fenrik do this dozens of times and was confident I could get it all situated while he bathed.

I could hear him in the water behind me, trying not to imagine his strong, thick body sitting in the tub as he soaped up. He'd been shirtless dozens of times and I'd memorized his heavy pectoral muscles and powerful stomach. He was built more like Hulk Hogan than Fabio, and I had no complaints. We were headed somewhere, but that path didn't involve me perving on him while he bathed. I heard him get out of the water and head to the bathroom, so I knew it was safe to start arranging the skewers on a tray to bring to the fire. I was startled as I felt Fenrik approach me and take in a deep breath of my hair before kissing the top of my head. I leaned into him, finding myself against a solid wall of muscle.

"Hi." I turned to him.

His wet hair was tied back, and he stood there in all his shirtless gloriousness. I thought about broaching the subject of our shared kiss but turned to the skewers I'd made. I sat down next to them on the low table while Fenrik took a seat on the couch across from me and leaned back. I started placing the skewers in the fire, as I had seen Fenrik do when he cleared his throat. He looked as nervous as I felt, with his hands clasped in his lap.

"This—kissing for you," he started.

"Yes?"

"It is difficult for you?" He looked concerned.

Difficult? No, kissing Fenrik was definitely not difficult.

"No. Kissing you is not a hardship." I understood what he was getting at, but I wanted to be clear: "Where I was raised, I was raised Christian—it's a religion in America. I was raised to be pure. I was only meant to have sex with my husband. I went to my wedding night with very little understanding of what was expected of me. With Gabe I spent quite a bit of time having sex that was... eh?"

To my surprise, Fenrik looked angry.

"Pure? For what reason?" he asked.

"Uhh, there was a Christian text that said couples should wait until marriage to be... intimate. A lot of that weight fell on the females because males were seen to lack self-control," I explained.

"So, you were expected to repress your own sexual appetite *and* control those of your partners?" he hissed.

"Well, yeah. The first boy I kissed blamed me for 'tempting him' into it." I thought of stupid Seth's face.

We'd done a lot more, and he'd made me feel like a sinner and a temptress every step of the way.

Fenrik studied me for a moment with pain in his eyes as he realized the consistent negative experiences I'd had.

"So you never got to figure out what you wanted? What you liked?"

"I mean, there are things I stumbled upon, like kissing," I said, grinning, "but no, exploration was frowned upon."

"Well, you realize there are no humans here, right? No one to judge you. And orkin definitely do not ascribe to this purity… whatever." His lip curled in disgust.

It was true. There was no one here. Not even other orcs. I could do whatever I wanted. My eyes got wide. Whatever I wanted? With a hot orc who was clearly interested in me. My brain was reeling. I could do *anything.* There was no one here to pass judgment or call me a whore or a temptress.

"I promise, there are no humans under the bed waiting to shame you for going after what you want," Fenrik said

"I'd wanted to fuck my first boyfriend at fifteen but was told it would damn me to hell," I blurted out.

Something about this line of questioning made me wanted to tell Fenrik the truth—my truth. "I had a really high libido for a teenage girl, and I had no idea how to deal with it. It all felt… wrong," I'd just laid my soul on the floor in front of Fenrik. I stared down at the floor with my face flaming. I had just trauma dumped all over this poor orc. *Jesus.*

Fenrik looked thoughtful for a moment—as if he was really considering what I was saying.

"What if you just did what you wanted? What is it you want?" Fenrik asked—with curiosity, not judgment. "Knowing that the only one here is me."

"I want everything. Everything I have been missing out on. Everything I have been ashamed to try. I want it all." All the words jumbled out before I had a chance to stop them. I was embarrassed but also so, so ready. I'd already trusted Fenrik with my life, my safety. My only hesitation about trusting him with my body was… did he want it too? I felt like he'd made that very clear.

"And when would you like to do this?"

"Now. Right now. I want it all right at this very moment," I said, throwing caution to the wind.

CHAPTER 10

While Tracy had said she wanted everything, I wasn't sure if now was the right time to tell her that I'd been able to smell her arousal over the last few weeks. Recently, it had gone from being every once in a while, especially when I was shirtless, to being constant. While it was doing wonders for my ego, other than the few kisses we'd shared, it hadn't progressed any further. Now that I had a better understanding as to why, I could at least try.

We sat beside each other, Tracy with her hands in her lap, fidgeting with her cuticles. I wasn't sure what to say. Intimacy wasn't usually discussed at this level. We were both ready to go but nervous to start.

"Do you want to touch me?" I asked hesitantly.

Immediately, Tracy drew a finger up one of my tusks, then the other. They were new to her, so it made sense for her to be curious about them, but she didn't stop there. She traced a single finger across my lower lip, causing a shudder to slip down my spine.

"Is this okay? Your lips are very soft." She traced my upper lip.

"So are yours." I pulled my lips into a smile.

"Do you want to do more kissing?" She paused her exploration.

"I would very much like to continue kissing. I find this human custom of pressing lips together fascinating," I teased.

The last time we kissed, it just happened. Now that we discussed it, figuring out how to start seemed much harder. My tusks felt much too large, and my tongue suddenly felt dry as a bone. But Tracy seemed sure as she used my tusks to pull me down to her before pressing her lips against mine. Then all concern about how to do this right flew out of my head. I remembered this. This felt amazing. Tracy didn't just stop at placing her lips on mine. She used her tongue to trace along the seam of my mouth, so I parted for her. She snaked her tongue in, exploring my mouth. She dragged her soft tongue along my textured one, causing my whole body to light up with want. I tangled my tongue with hers, attempting to explore every part of her mouth. She was so soft everywhere. I slid my tongue across her tiny, blunted teeth and the inside of her cheeks. A small moan escaped her.

I wanted her closer. I wanted to touch more of her. We were still sitting beside each other, our hands in our respective laps. I would be able to kiss so much more of her if we were facing each other completely, but I didn't want to push her. I pulled away.

"Can I… can I put my hands around your waist?" I asked.

"How about something a little more?"

I nodded vigorously, wondering what she had in mind.

She flung her leg over my lap, straddling my waist, and devoured my lips, threading her fingers through my hair.

While it was unexpected and amazing to have her petite frame so close to mine, I was very aware that she would be able to feel my arousal in this position, and I didn't want to frighten her.

I pulled back for a moment. "I… um… I can't control my cock when we are kissing."

"I would be offended if you could." She grinned and ground against my lap.

Well, that was one less thing to worry about.

"Do you like this?"

"More. I want more." There wasn't another thought in my head. I wanted to sink into her, knot and all. And have her bear my young. *Fuck, what was I thinking?* Going slow with Tracy was going to test every ounce of my willpower.

"Then you'll have more," she teased.

"Are you sure?" I cocked my head to the side, studying her. Her cheeks were flushed pink, and her lips were swollen from our enthusiastic kissing.

"I don't know if I will be able to stop once we start." She kissed me again. "That's what always got me in trouble back home. I was never satisfied."

"Can I—can I see your chest? Would me teasing your nipples feel good?"

Tracy blinked at me.

"Um… I don't actually know. But I am comfortable with trying?" she said, flushing a deeper shade of pink.

"You don't need to be embarrassed. I want to try everything with you, and I know some of it will be new." I pulled her in for another kiss.

She reached up, slid the straps of her pink dress down to expose her chest. It was as perfect as I had imagined it. Her breasts were pert and small and even paler than the rest of her, each tipped with pebbled pink nipples. I wanted to take each one of them into my mouth and suckle on her until she screamed. Was that something humans did? She seemed unfamiliar with the idea but open to it.

"These are perfect. You are perfect." I trailed a finger down from her collarbone to the tip of her hardened nipple. Tracy let out a gasp. "Did that feel good?"

She nodded vigorously but said nothing as I continued to tease at her nipple with my thumb. The smell of her arousal was intoxicating and growing by the second. I massaged both of her breasts and dragging my thumbs back and forth across her nipples, earning me another moan.

I brought my mouth to one of Tracy's nipples and flicked my tongue across it before suckling it as if I could draw milk from her. It was perfect and delicious, and I wanted to devour her whole. The taste of her skin was like a drug that I could never get enough of. As I sucked at her nipple, I felt Tracy stiffen and then arch her chest into me. She grabbed me by my hair and pulled me closer. Oh, she liked this. I continued to torment her one nipple with my tongue before switching to the next.

"Fenrik, that feels…" She stopped, unable to complete her thought with me latched on her nipple.

I laved at her stiff peaks, dragging my tongue up and down as she shuddered beneath me. I pulled back and tweaked each of her nipples gently between my thumbs and forefingers, causing her to look at me wide-eyed, mouth in a perfect O.

"Is this too much?" I asked.

"No—no. I… holy bananas, I had no idea I could get so turned on by someone playing with those."

I had no idea what bananas were, but she seemed pleased, so I returned my mouth to her chest, tonguing each of her nipples thoroughly.

"Can I—can I touch you?" she asked breathlessly.

I released her breast with a pop, looking up at her blue eyes. "Wherever you want," I said, voice husky.

She reached down between us and stroked the length of my cock over my pants. She dragged her fingers up and down, learning the size of me, and her eyes widened again.

"Most of my experience has been with my ex's penis before, but… I would very much like to see yours," she said.

The hitch in her voice nearly killed me. I wanted to strangle the man who had done this to her.

TRACY

I'd played with my own nipples when I was young. My mom always slapped my hand away, telling me it was inappropriate. I was barely a pre-teen. Gabe never really paid attention to my nipples, happy to massage my breasts to suit his own needs. Fenrik's attention made me feel like I would combust at any moment. Could a person come from nipple play alone? I had no idea. What I did know was that I was dripping wet and wanted more. I'd never even experienced wetness like this. Gabe and I had used lube, which I hated. It made me feel like I was riding a slip-and-slide.

I reached my hands between us and started to unlace Fenrik's pants. I wasn't sure where we'd stop, but I didn't care. I wanted more and more of him. I shoved his pants down, pulling out his cock between us. Definitely not a human cock. I leaned back to get a good look at it. It was a darker green than the rest of his skin. It was textured, with a pattern that almost looked braided and a large bulge at the base. I wondered how that would fit. I stroked my fingers along the ridges of his cock, learning it. It was huge. Though it was much larger than I was used to, I was ready and willing. Maybe we would have to work up to it?

I dragged my fingers up and down the braided ridges, earning me a groan from Fenrik. He also appeared to be uncircumcised, which I guess made sense but was new to me. I wondered what it might be like to lick his foreskin but reined myself in. We needed to take this slow. But then the quiet part in the back of my brain said, why? Why do I need to take this slow? There was no one here to judge me for riding Fenrik until I came screaming his name.

I wrapped my hand around his textured cock, my fingers unable to meet due to his girth. I pumped him up and down, surprised to find the extra skin meant I could easily give him a hand job without lube. I found myself salivating. A hand job would not be enough. I stroked down his cock again, pulling the foreskin back to expose his leaking tip, looking at him to gauge his reaction. Fenrik looked at me, slack-jawed.

"Are you sure you are comfortable touching me like this? Because I assure you, if you continue you are going to have a mess all over your hands."

"Very sure," I responded, keeping my fingers wrapped around his length. "I think I've proven I can handle a little mess." I smirked.

I wondered briefly if I could fit his cock in my mouth. I continued stroking him while pulling him into a kiss. We devoured each other. I wanted to know where we could go with this, and my brain was telling me *all the way*, but I was trying to keep myself in check. I nibbled at his lips while I dragged my hand up and down his shaft, relishing the textured feel of his hot skin under my hand. These ridges would feel amazing during sex. I wanted him to fuck me now. There was no one here to tell me it was against God's will or whatever the fuck excuse they made for keeping women pure. Fenrik pulled away from our kiss.

"Can I—can I touch you as well?" he asked uncertainly.

I had never had someone use their hands on me *there*. I wasn't sure what to expect, but I trusted Fenrik. I nodded vigorously, wondering what was in store. He continued to kiss my neck and jaw as he pushed up my dress. I had no underwear on because I only had the one pair I'd arrived in— I'd stopped bothering. He slid his hand all the way up my thigh, gently dragging his fingers along my curls.

Part of my brain was yelling at me to be embarrassed by having pubic hair and being dripping wet. The other part of me told me to lean into it. He wouldn't have asked to do this if he didn't want to. I kissed Fenrik, trying to calm the riot in my head. Fenrik reached my dripping folds and drew a finger up and down them, causing me to squirm in his lap. He used his fingers to split me open, finding my clit easily. I gasped as he brushed against it.

"Does that feel good?"

"It feels… good and too much all at once," I said, my voice wavering.

"Okay, I can make this work." He continued stroking me.

He circled my clit without touching it directly, causing me to light up in ways I didn't know were possible. Fenrik gently circled my clit with his thumb and then pressed two fingers into me, and I let out a gasp. He pumped his fingers in and out of me while continuing to circle my clit. I felt as if I would lose consciousness from the pleasure. The attention to my clit while filling me with his fingers was enough to bring me to the brink. I'd never orgasmed with a partner, which I assumed was normal. Yet here I was, on the edge, with only Fenrik's fingers.

"Fenrik, it's too much—" I gasped.

"Do you want me to stop?"

"No—er—whoa, no. Don't stop." My brain was scrambled by the onslaught of sensations.

Fenrik continued delving into me with his thick fingers, all while circling my clit with his thumb. I couldn't control my panting as he worked me, feeling as if I couldn't get enough air into my lungs. Then, all of a sudden, all of my muscles locked down, and I was coming and coming and coming.

"What have you done to me, Fenrik?" I slurred, drunken on my own pleasure.

"I'm tending to your needs," he said simply, without changing the rhythm or the motion he was using on my clit and wet channel.

My vision blurred as I came, unable to deal with the freight train of pleasure that was barreling into me. I gasped for air as Fenrik brought me down, holding me gently, as if he knew this was an entirely new experience for me.

CHAPTER 11

TRACY

Fenrik was a drug that I wanted more of. I sat limply in his lap, boneless from the orgasm that just rocked my world. I had no idea that this is what intimacy could be like. As he continued to kiss down my neck, I realized that I'd finished and he hadn't. I reached down between us to stroke his still-hard cock.

"Hey, hey, we don't have to do this if you aren't ready," he said softly.

"You just gave me what I believe was my first orgasm with a partner, and you expect me not to reciprocate?" I looked at him, brow cocked.

"I have no expectations. Seeing you come undone by me was enough. I look forward to doing it many times over."

"Well. It would please me to see you come undone the way I just did," I said nervously—I wasn't used to being so open—but if there was a time to be honest, it was now.

"I would be more than willing to do that." He run his

fingers through my hair. "But seeing you come was enough for me."

"Can I—would you like it if I sucked your cock?" I asked shyly.

"Is that something that humans do?" He sounded surprised.

"Most definitely. It's something I am rather fond of, even with history taken into consideration," I said with a grin.

I imagined with my feelings toward Fenrik it would be even more exciting. I took hold of his cock again, but didn't stroke him—waiting for permission.

"If it is truly something you want to do, I am open to trying," he said, looking skeptical.

"I promise. You aren't pressuring me into anything," I whispered as I slid down his lap and onto my knees in front of him.

I gripped his cock with both hands. There was no way I could fit the entire thing into my mouth. This would have to be a blowjob and hand job combo. Luckily for me, I was a pro at both.

"Can we pull your pants down a bit more? I want better access." I peered up at him through my lashes.

Fenrik stood and pulled his pants all the way off, exposing his thick thighs and hairy legs. For the love of God, who ever thought I'd be turned on by leg hair? Fenrik was so... *rugged* in a way I wasn't used to. I knelt in front of him as he settled back down on the couch, his giant alien cock at attention.

I gripped his shaft, unsure of what to do with the bulbous protrusion at the base. I took the head of his cock into my mouth while firmly gripping the base with my hand. The taste of his precum was... unexpected. It was slightly sweet, like nothing I'd experienced before. I was only able to draw the head into my mouth while I wished I could detach my jaw and devour him whole.

I dragged my tongue along the length of the underside of his cock, earning me a tortured groan. This. This is what I loved. I continued to stroke him while alternating between licking him like a popsicle and sucking all that I could take. I wanted to see him explode. I thought of all the ways he had provided for me in the past weeks—no questions asked—and was spurred on. I wanted this orc to come like he'd never come before.

I used both hands, one on his shaft, the other massaging his balls, which were covered in silky black hair. Fenrik let out a noise that could only be described as a growl, and I knew I was on the right track. I popped off his cock, breathlessly.

"What is this?" I asked, gripping the bulge near the base of his cock.

"It's my knot," he said, breathing hard. "If we fuck it will lock us together to ensure you receive all of my cum into your cunt."

"Does it feel good when I touch it?" I asked, gripping it tightly.

"Yes—yes, it does. Fuck, Tracy. It is more than I ever thought," he gasped.

I loved this. Maybe I was inexperienced, but I was the pro when it came to kissing and blowjobs. I was going to give him the blowjob of a lifetime. I sucked and licked and dragged my palm up and down his cock, all earning me earnest groans.

"Tracy, I can't hold back much longer," he said, voice ragged.

I paused working him momentarily. "Then come in my mouth."

He looked at me agog. "Are you sure?"

"Very sure," I said, resuming licking his cock while massaging his knot and his balls with my hands.

He was holding his breath in a way that I knew combustion was inevitable. I doubled my efforts, dragging my tongue along the sensitive skin underneath his foreskin. Fenrik gasped and moved to put his fingers through my hair but stopped himself.

"You can maneuver me however you'd like. I'd love it," I said between licks. I had taken to licking him up and then swirling my tongue around the tip like an ice cream cone.

Without a word, he wound my hair in his fingers and pulled me toward him. I happily opened wide and took him as deeply as I could. I groaned with satisfaction so Fenrik would know I was enjoying this almost as much as he was. His cock and his cum tasted marvelous. If this continued, Fenrik would be getting blowjobs daily. I felt him thicken as he reached his peak and sucked him down even harder, all while still tending to his knot and shaft with my hands.

"Tracy—" was all he got out before he exploded in my mouth.

I was used to cum, but this was a lot of cum. I swallowed every bit that I could before releasing him and letting him come across my face. This was, hands down, the best blowjob I had ever given. Being covered in Fenrik's sticky-sweet cum was almost more than I could handle. It covered my lips and jaw and dripped down onto my chest. Orcs came by the bucketload. Noted.

As Fenrik finished and noticed my cum-covered face, his expression went from ecstasy to mortification.

"Fenrik, it's fine. I loved it. Get me a cloth, and we're good to go," I reassured him.

He ran to the restroom, and I could hear the water running. He brought me a damp washcloth to wipe my face and chest. He was naked, and I was topless, and all I wanted to do was curl up together and bask in our "first time." He wiped my face and breasts tenderly, cleaning every part of me.

"Just so you know, I will never be upset about being covered in your cum," I said as he wiped my chin.

He blushed but said nothing as he continued to clean me.

"What now?" I was still on my knees in front of him.

"You go to bed, and I sleep on the couch?" He hesitated. I could almost see the process he was trying to go through to figure out where we went from here.

"No. We're going to have sex. Very soon. I want you in bed with me, wrapped around my body."

Fenrik looked pleased but shocked.

"You sleep with me from now on," I said emphatically. "Can orcs—do you need a resting period before you cum again?"

"No, I can fill you with my cum over and over again." He had a hungry look on his face.

As marvelous as that sounded, it sent my mind screeching to a halt. "Uh… do you have any way of preventing pregnancy?" One reason I ran was that I wasn't about to have a baby I didn't want. As much as I wanted to sleep with Fenrik, the idea of babies terrified me.

"Oh, yes. We do. It's tea. We'd need to forage for the leaves." He stood quickly, pulling on his pants and boots and looking out the window. "I'll be back as soon as I can."

"Wh-What?" I wrung my hands in confusion. Was he leaving now? In the middle of… this?

"Do you want to have sex?" he asked, voice husky.

I just nodded vigorously, eyes wide.

"Well, then I am going to find some leaves so I can make you some damn tea. Get in bed. Do you want me to wake you when I return?" He pulled his tunic and cloak on.

"Yes. Yes, definitely wake me." I stood, with my dress still scrunched up around my waist.

Fenrik pulled me into him, nuzzling my temple, then kissing down my neck.

"Can you take this off before you get in bed?" He tugged at my dress.

"Mmmm," I mumbled in agreement, pulling him in for a kiss.

He pulled away and cupped my cheek with his hand. "I will be back as soon as I can."

And with that, he was off, and I was alone in the cabin, utterly exposed. I headed to the bedroom, yanking my dress off as I walked. The room was pleasantly warm, thanks to the fire that Fenrik always kept crackling for me. I slid into the bed, naked, determined to stay awake until Fenrik returned.

I lay on my side, replaying the events of the evening. We hadn't even eaten dinner. I found that I didn't care. I dragged my fingers along the soft bedding and absentmindedly wondered how long it would take to forage for leaves. I hoped not long. The sun was already starting to set.

I smiled to myself at the thought of Fenrik returning to find me naked in our now shared bed, and anxiety reared its ugly head. I had no doubts about sleeping with Fenrik, but unraveling my upbringing wasn't going to come in a single night.

I calmed, reminding myself that it was only me and Fenrik in the cabin, miles away from any orcs and galaxies away from Earth. I was free. Freer than I ever thought I would be.

I slowly drifted to sleep as I relished that freedom, wondering what it would be like to do whatever I wanted, whenever I wanted.

FENRIK

I would have to work quickly in the fading light to find tea leaves. I should have thought to do this sooner, but up until tonight, it seemed presumptive. Now, I needed leaves, and I needed them quickly. Luckily, with my mom being the tribe's herbalist, I knew what to look for. The leaves grew in the shade of the trees that lined the stream. I practically sprinted to the water. It took a few trees before I found one of the herb bushes. It was thriving, so I took only enough leaves for the next several days and left the rest, noting where the bush was so I could return. I knew that female orkin wishing to prevent pregnancy needed to drink it daily.

I hurried back to the cabin in the dark, as the sun had set while I was foraging. I opened the back door quietly. After depositing the leaves on the counter, I started to boil the water before checking on Tracy. She was fast asleep in the bed.

My brain bounced back and forth as to whether I should wake her. She did tell me to, but she looked so peaceful. She sighed and rolled over in her sleep, revealing her bare breasts. Decision made.

I returned to the kitchen, removed the water from the heat, and threw in a handful of leaves. It needed to steep until it was a bright green color. I started to pull my clothes off as the tea brewed, including my boots, then my tunic. I decided to keep my pants on. I didn't want to wake her up with the tea and my hard cock directly in her eyeline.

After what seemed like an eternity, the tea turned into the expected brilliant shade of green. I carefully poured a cup of it into an earthenware mug and headed to the bedroom, blowing on it so it would be cool enough for Tracy to drink.

Tracy was curled on her side, sleeping, as I sat down on the end of the bed. I stroked her thigh gently through the blankets, not wanting her to startle.

"Fenrik?" she mumbled sleepily.

"Já, I found the tea," I said, still touching her thigh.

Tracy's eyes snapped open, and she sat up immediately, causing some hot tea to spill over my hand and legs. I winced at the burning liquid but held my hand as still as possible.

"Oh god, I'm so sorry," Tracy cried, seeing me now covered in tea.

With my free hand, I waved off her concern. "Don't worry, there is still plenty for you to drink. That's all that matters." I gingerly passed her the mug.

She took it with both hands and smelled it. She scrunched up her nose. "It smells like black licorice."

"Is that a good thing or a bad thing?" I guessed licorice was a human thing.

"It's not terrible. Black licorice is a human candy that is an acquired taste. It could be worse," she said, blowing on the tea before taking a sip. She pursed her lips, thinking. "It's not terrible. I have to drink this every day?"

"Every day that you don't want an orkling." I laughed, trying to lighten this very serious conversation.

She took another sip, looking me up and down. "It's worth it," she whispered with a little grin.

I was slowly peeling away Tracy's layers and lived for her mischievous smile. Knowing that it was just for me felt like sliding into a tub of warm water. I watched her dutifully drink the tea for a few moments. My gaze roamed down to her bare chest, and I felt my cock throb in my pants and stood.

"Where are you going?" Tracy asked.

"Just to get more wood for the fire. I can't have my tiny human getting cold," I growled, standing and heading into the living room. I gathered a large stack and returned, tending to the fire while she finished her tea, eyes on me the entire time.

She finished, set her mug on the bedside table, and looked at me expectantly. There was no hiding the tent in my pants, and I could smell her arousal spiking as she chewed on her lower lip.

Now that it was here, I couldn't help but be nervous. We'd talked about this. We'd agreed to this. But it was still a big step. Everything that fell together naturally when we started kissing now felt weighty.

"Well, if I am going to be naked, you could, maybe, also be naked?" She hesitated. "I mean if you still want to do this."

The uncertainty in her voice snapped something inside of me. I would make Tracy feel absolutely cherished if it was the last thing I did. I stripped off my leggings and joined her under the covers. I lay on my side and pulled her to me so we could face each other. I nuzzled her temple and kissed down her neck hungrily, living for her scent. Tracy remained still for only a few seconds before sliding her hand into the hair at the nape of my neck and pressing her body against mine. I groaned, feeling my length trapped between our bodies and pressing into her soft stomach. I paused kissing her neck and pulled her face close to mine.

"Hi" was all she said.

"Hi yourself," I teased.

"Are you ready for our first time?" she chewed on her lip.

"If you are, I most certainly am." I ground my hips against her to reinforce my readiness.

"Yes. Yes. I want you. I want this." She pulled me in, finally kissing me again—firm and with intention. "But how?"

"Why don't you pick?" I started kissing down her neck again. I would take her in whatever way she wanted me to.

"Can you be on top? I don't have much experience running the show," she whispered, cheeks turning pink.

"Happily. But I need to make sure you are wet and ready for me, or I'm afraid I won't fit." I slid my hand down her soft skin to the thatch of hair covering her mound.

Slipping my hand further, I spread her damp folds, causing the scent of her arousal to further invade my nostrils. I stroked her, as I did before, circling my thumb around her sensitive clit, without touching it directly. She was already soaked for me. I continued circling her clit and slowly dipped one finger inside of her. I groaned as I slid one finger in and out of her, moving easily with how wet she was. She felt divine. I locked eyes with her as I continued to work my finger deeper.

"Fenrik, it's so—" She stopped, closing her eyes and bucking her hips into my hand.

I continued my pace circling her clit, adding pressure. I slid another finger into her tight channel, marveling as she mewled and squirmed. She was so sensitive. I pushed both fingers in and out, never letting up on her clit.

"Tracy, I am going to add a third finger," I whispered into her hair as she twitched under me.

"I think—I think I'm close?" she panted.

"Can you handle more?" I stroked her cheek with one hand and explored her with the other. I wanted her to come so she would be able to take me fully.

"Mmm" was all I got out of her as she continued to buck into my hand. I took that as a yes.

Adding a third finger made for an even tighter fit and I looked for signs of distress or pain on Tracy's face. Her pink mouth formed a perfect O, and her eyes were scrunched closed.

"Oh, oh, that's—oh, don't stop," she gasped.

I upped my pace, easily sliding three fingers in and out of her, making a slurping noise with each thrust in and out. I felt my cock grow impossibly harder as I watched my fingers slip in and out of her wetness. I wished I was guiding my cock into her dripping cunt, but Tracy came first. She pulled me closer, her tiny nails digging into my shoulders. She buried her face in my neck, and her breath was coming rapidly, hot on my neck, as she approached her climax. I kept my pace steady and used my free hand to massage her breast, knowing how sensitive her nipples were. I plucked at each of them, admiring their perfect light pink shade. They were completely alien to me and completely perfect. I dipped my head to bring one of them into my mouth, dragging my textured tongue across her stiff peak.

Tracy's grip on my shoulders tightened almost painfully as she locked up and her swollen channel clamped down on my fingers as she came screaming my name and garbled nonsense I barely understood.

"Stop, stop, it's too much." She pulled away.

I slid my fingers out of her slowly, trying not to overstimulate her. She was flushed pink all over and shaking.

"How was that?" I asked, using my free hand to brush her hair out of her face.

Tracy's eyes were wide in disbelief. "I didn't know my body could do that. That was… a lot."

"Good a lot or bad a lot?" I stopped touching her.

"Oh, good a lot, definitely good a lot." She reached out to me, and I watched her take note of the little crescent moon marks she'd left while digging her nails into my shoulders.

"Fenrik, I'm so sorry. Did I hurt you?" Her face was twisted up with concern.

I laughed. As if Tracy could hurt me. "No, I didn't even feel it. I was too focused on you coming undone. You are beautiful when you come."

Tracy flushed an even deeper shade of pink. "Um… thank you?"

She stopped twitching, and her breath started to even out as she came down, so I wrapped my arms around her and pressed her into me, nuzzling into her neck.

"You are amazing," I whispered into her ear before licking up the shell of it.

FENRIK

$\mathcal{I}$ shifted so I was on top of her. Her eyes were hooded with lust, and she smelled incredible. It was taking all of my restraint to prevent me from ramming myself into her. I spread her thighs to accommodate my hips, and she followed willingly. She wrapped her legs around my waist and pulled me in for a kiss, causing my cock to jump against her. I parted my lips so our tongues could tangle together.

I moved my hips against hers, lining myself up at her entrance, before pausing to check in with her one last time. I pulled away from our kiss and stared down at her. She didn't look nervous or afraid. She looked *hungry*.

"Last chance to change your mind," I said through gritted teeth, holding myself back with every fiber of my being.

"Never." She gave an adorable little growl before enthusiastically kissing me again.

I slowly started pressing into her tight heat, sliding in less than halfway before I paused and pulled out. I thrust shallowly, willing her to open for me. I was determined to go slow for her, but Tracy wasn't having any of it. She wrapped her legs more tightly around my waist, pulling my cock deeper, silently asking for more. She was such a small thing, astounded at her body's ability to accommodate me. I watched her face for signs of concern or pain, but I saw shock and pleasure. I pumped in and out of her at a steady pace, letting her continue to grow accustomed to me. Her tight cunt was driving me insane, and I longed to thrust my knot into her. It bumped up against her pussy with every perfect thrust. She arched her back, meeting me stroke for stroke.

"Can I—can I go deeper?" I hesitated.

Tracy pressed her lips to mine and dragged her hands down to my ass, pulling me deeper.

"I want all of you," she murmured as she locked eyes with me.

I sunk in even deeper, readying her for my knot. She was dripping wet, but I knew the knot would be unexpected for her.

"Do you think you can take my knot?"

She nodded vigorously, splaying her hips even wider. I pressed into her further, feeling my knot breach her core. She shuddered underneath me.

"Is it too much?" I asked, trying to keep myself tethered.

"No—it is—it is a lot, but a lot good," she panted.

With all her tentativeness and inexperience, I never expected to be here, in bed, with Tracy. And now here she was, taking my knot. She was incredible.

"Can we keep going?" She wound her fingers through my hair and pulled me to her lips.

I kissed her deeply as I pistoned my hips, feeling my knot drag along her sensitive channel with each stroke. I wedged my hand between us, reaching for her clit. I wanted another orgasm out of her before I came. I found her clit and circled it with my thumb. My knot was making obscene noises as I thrust in and out of her, but she only pulled me closer, devouring my lips and my neck. I was close, but she was going to come first. I slowed my pace, focusing on circling her clit with the pad of my thumb.

"Fenrik, it's too much," she gasped.

"Lean into it." I took her earlobe gently between my teeth and sucked it.

"I don't know if I can," she cried. "I feel like I am going to pee all over you."

"Then you'll pee all over me. I just came on your face. I see no difference," I assured her.

She looked at me nervously but nodded, giving me permission to keep stroking her clit while I thrust in and out of her. I ratcheted up my pace while keeping the circles around her clit steady and adding more pressure. I watched her, ensuring it wasn't too much, but she gripped me harder, digging her fingers into my shoulders and locking her legs around my waist. I felt her tighten up on me, her finish approaching, just as I felt the tingling of mine at the base of my spine.

She clamped down on me, moaning my name. I was so close. I thrust once more as Tracy came with muscles locking up, letting out a string of garbled words I couldn't make sense of. The sensation of her tightening up around me was too much, and I unleashed a torrent of cum inside her, my vision blurring with pleasure. I leaned to the side as I collapsed so I didn't crush my tiny human, vaguely wondering when I had started thinking of her as *mine*. All this time at the cabin, Tracy had started to feel like home. Now that we were in the same bed at night, I wanted nothing more than to stay by her side.

I rolled us so we could face each other, still locked together. We lay like that for several quiet moments, lazily stroking each other.

"How long are we..." She looked down to where our bodies were joined.

"Only a few moments." I stroked her hair, trying to figure out what she was thinking. "Was that... is this too much?"

"Too much?" Her voice pitched up in surprise. "No, no, no.... definitely not too much." She peppered my face all over with kisses. "I just..." She averted her eyes.

"Just what? You don't have to be embarrassed or ashamed of anything in front of me. And you didn't even pee on me."

Tracy snorted. "I'm definitely not worried about that. I was wondering if once we are... unlocked or whatever you call it," she said, waving her hand at where we were joined, "if after we could... um..."

I raised my brows, waiting for her to spit it out. I would help her, but I had no idea what she was *wondering*.

"If we could?" I prompted her.

"If we could do this again," she mumbled almost too quietly for me to hear.

That was not what I expected. Tracy still had her eyes averted and her head turned in embarrassment. I took her chin and gently turned her face so she had to look at me. She was no longer tinged pink with the exertion of our fucking. She was bright red with embarrassment. She was worrying her lip again as she made eye contact with me.

"Tracy, I know this is all very different from what you are used to, but I would love nothing more than to go again." I pulled her closer to me, resting my head on top of hers. "I don't know what human males are like, but male orcs can come repeatedly." I murmured into her hair.

I felt the walls of Tracy's warm channel clench around my

cock as she hugged me tightly, clamping down even further on my knot.

"Okay, but you can't do that, or I will never soften enough to pull out," I groaned with pleasure.

Tracy released me and went very still. "I think I can keep my hands to myself… for a few minutes." She smirked.

What have I unlocked in this quiet, sad human?

Tracy

I was surprised to wake up tangled up with Fenrik, arms and legs draped over each other. Then I remembered the night before and grinned. Fenrik had not only fucked me within an inch of my life—he'd done it twice. I'd lost count of orgasms. I was actually starting to wonder if the previous orgasms I'd had before even counted. They felt like just blips of heightened pleasure compared to the mind-blowing orgasms Fenrik had given me. I was tempted to wake him and demand round three, but that seemed selfish. Now that I knew what sex could be, I felt insatiable. He *did* say he could go again and again. Maybe he wouldn't mind being woken up by a blowjob, I thought wickedly. I gently unwrapped myself from him, letting him lie on his back. His cock was already semi-hard, morning wood and all. I was drooling at the sight of it. The tip of his cock was just poking out of his foreskin.

I examined it briefly before licking his cock from root to tip, taking his penis into my mouth and dragging my tongue along it.

He shuddered awake as I sucked his cockhead. "Again?" he asked huskily.

"Absolutely."

Saying nothing, he grabbed me and placed me on my

hands and knees. Oh, this was new. Fenrik pushed me down so my face made contact with the pillows, exposing me completely. I expected him to fuck me immediately, but he took his time. He spread me wide, and I felt his fingers spread my lips and then gasped as his tongue made contact with my clit. I stiffened.

"Whoa, whoa, whoa," I gasped in shock.

Fenrik looked alarmed as he straightened up. "Is this something that you aren't comfortable with?" He raised his hands in the air in what I guessed was the universal signal for *I mean no harm.*

I shifted to sit in front of him on the bed, and he sat beside me. "I honestly don't know. I've never had it done."

"So you had done this for your husband many times over, and he never once reciprocated?" he asked, grimacing.

I felt my cheeks get hot with shame. "Um, a lot of guys on Earth, or I guess where I am from, treat it like a chore? So I never asked."

"Tracy, what did you say to me last night?"

"Probably a whole lot of unintelligible nonsense. You nearly fucked the life out of me." I laughed.

"No. Before that. You told me you *enjoyed* giving me pleasure—expecting nothing in return. You wake me up with your lips around my cock but don't expect me to want to do the same?"

I was really at a loss. I didn't know what to say to that very logical thought process. It just wasn't the way things were done. "Well, when you put it that way, it makes the whole thing sound stupid." I twisted my fingers in my lap, staring at them.

"It *is* stupid," he said emphatically. "How did you feel when I came in your mouth and all over you? I don't even need to ask. You told me you *loved* seeing me undone and being covered in my seed. Why wouldn't I want to do the same?"

He stroked a warm palm down my thigh, resting his hand on my knee. It was the anchor I needed. I grasped his hand in mine.

The truth of the situation felt even stupider now that he'd explained it from his perspective. "Well, where I am from, a woman is taught to... tend to her husband's needs. Before last night, I'd only ever been fingered a few times and am not sure if I ever orgasmed." I shrugged.

Fenrik looked disgusted and exasperated, dragging a hand over his face. "Tracy, can I lick you?"

"Do you want to?" I scrunched up my face in embarrassment.

"Do I want to lick your delectable cunt and finally taste your arousal that I have been smelling for days and days and watch you completely shatter?" He cocked his head, looking at me like I was an idiot.

"You can smell me?!" I gasped, mortified, thinking of every time I had grown wet just by looking at the corded muscles of his arms or the line of his jaw.

"Yes. But before we had our conversation about your fear of *judgment*, but not a fear of *intimacy*, I didn't want to act on it if you weren't ready," he said, gripping my hand before letting go.

I put my face in my hands. This was all so messed up. Stupid Christianity. Stupid patriarchy. Stupid. Stupid. I felt my eyes start to well up.

"Hey, hey." Fenrik grabbed my hands and pulled me into his lap. "I didn't ask, I assumed. I didn't know."

He kissed away my tears. "I just didn't think that my tongue would be an issue, considering we've already had sex."

"No, no." I shook my head. "That makes complete sense. You had no way of knowing."

"Can we just take everything you learned about sex and intimacy and burn it to the ground?" he whispered into my hair.

"Um… I might take a little longer than that to get used to it, but I'm up for trying," I said, voice wobbly.

"Then, let's start with this. In orkin culture, males love pleasuring their mates with their tongues. They want to see them come from their mouth alone at least once before having sex. Not only do we enjoy it, we use it to ready you for our cocks. We want you dripping before we try to slide into you, considering the knot and all. I want to latch onto your delectable cunt and drink down your juices while you come screaming."

"That is… well… I'm not even sure what to do with that," I said, eyes wide in shock.

Not only had he just used the word cunt, but he had called mine delectable. I blinked at him several times. There was no way he was lying about how much he wanted to devour me.

"Can we try again?" he asked gently.

"You're still in the mood even after all of this?"

"I can tell you are." He smirked.

I smacked his arm. "You know, that really isn't fair."

He responded by pulling my legs out from under me and spreading me flat on my back. He bent each of my knees, spreading me wide open. He had me laid out on the bed like a starfish and I'd never felt more exposed. He stared at me for a long time, so long that I started to feel uncomfortable. I went to pull my legs together, and he stopped me.

"Your pink cunt is as perfect as the rest of you." He reached out and dragged a finger up my slit, causing me to squirm.

"Well, I shall file that away as the weirdest compliment I have ever received." I snorted.

He continued his exploration of me with his hands, almost lazy in his movements. Using his thumb and forefinger, he spread me wide.

"Can we try this again?" he asked.

I nodded. Knowing he truly wanted this made me want to make him happy. Even if I wasn't sure if I would like it, the idea of someone's face in my crotch was still a bit alarming. He wedged his shoulders between my thighs and bent down, dragging his tongue across my clit.

"Too much, too much!" I squealed.

The onslaught of sensation was overwhelming. I felt like a live wire. He pulled back and looked at me quizzically.

"Let me try something slightly different."

He leaned in again, and instead of dragging the flat of his textured tongue across my clit, he circled it gently with the tip.

"Oh. Oh, that is—oh my. Yes," I stuttered.

It was enough sensation to light me up but not overwhelm me. Fenrik wrapped his warm hands around my thighs and continued using his tongue in the same circular motions. I was completely exposed to him and tried focusing on the feeling, not thinking about his face on my pubes. I dug my hands into his hair as he lavished attention on me. The way he dragged his tongue across my clit made me tingle all over, but it wasn't enough; I needed something more.

"Fenrik, fingers, please." I couldn't even bear to say the whole sentence, but I knew what I needed now.

Fenrik immediately slid two of his fingers inside while he still circled my clit with his tongue. I couldn't hold back the pants and moans as he stroked me. I was on the verge of combusting, but with all the panting, I was dying.

"Water," I gasped, "I need water."

Fenrik grasped a glass from the bedside and handed it to me. I gulped it down as he continued to work me. He added a third finger, pushing in and out of me while still using his mouth on my clit. Now that he'd readied me, he dragged the flat of his tongue across my clit again. This time, instead of feeling like too much, it felt amazing.

My legs clamped around him. "Yes, yes, don't stop," I moaned.

He continued to pump in and out of me with three fingers. At this point, I was so wet that every time he slid his fingers in, it made sloppy, wet noises. He didn't let up on my clit, and I felt myself begin to tighten, climax impending.

"Come for me, my little kyrr," Fenrik growled.

I grabbed his hair even harder, pressing my thighs into his shoulders. He continued his steady movements as I crested my peak, screaming his name.

"Fenrik, oh holy hell. Oh, it's so good!" I keened.

Nothing had prepared me for sex to be like this. Fenrik reared up and licked my juices off of each one of his fingers as if it was the most delicious thing he'd ever tasted.

"Now I have prepared you properly," he said, climbing over me.

He buried his face in my neck and kissed and licked down my collarbone before heading for my nipple. Knowing how much I had enjoyed this before, I was giddy with anticipation. Fenrik pulled a nipple into his mouth, lightly biting down on it with his teeth before flicking it with the tip of his tongue. I was literally dripping with anticipation. Now I understood why orcs put so much emphasis on oral pleasure.

"Fenrik," I breathed as he sucked on my nipples alternately, "I need your cock and I need it now."

He looked up at me with a mischievous grin. "So you enjoyed my tongue on you?"

I nodded rapidly as he climbed up, kissing me everywhere

as he went. When he reached my mouth, I was surprised at how erotic the taste of me on his tongue felt.

"Can we try something different?" he asked.

"Absolutely. I think you've earned my trust," I said, wondering what he had in mind.

He repositioned me so I was lying on my side, with him spooning me, cock pressing against my ass.

"I like this position because I can explore you while I fuck you," he said, dragging his hand across my breast, pinching my nipple.

"Are you sure you can fit this way?"

"There's only one way to find out," he said, a tinge of laughter in his voice.

Fenrik wrapped his much larger body around mine but pulled up my thigh so he could reach my entrance. He slid his cockhead up and down my slit before slowly pressing into me and releasing my leg. Oh, this position could work. It could work well. Fenrik started with slow, shallow thrusts, as we figured out fucking while spooning. It was a tight fit with my legs locked together, but the drag of his cock in and out of me had me seeing stars. Between this position and the oral I'd already received, I was going to combust at any moment.

"Fenrik, I've already come. You do whatever you need to finish," I said, voice thick.

Coming first was brand new to me, and I didn't want Fenrik to feel he needed to do more to please me.

"Oh, I'm going to make you come again before that," he murmured.

I reached my hand back and dragged my hands through his hair as he continued to pump in and out of me. He'd already loosened me, so I was close to being ready for his knot.

"Harder, Fenrik, *harder*. Give me your knot," I begged, pressing my ass into him each time he thrust into me.

Fenrik wrapped his arms around my waist and pulled me even closer to him. Even in this position, I could feel his knot pumping up against my entrance with every thrust. I spread my hips wider, allowing him better access, and his knot plunged into me. I gasped at the onslaught of sensations, realizing that although I thought I was at my limit, I could definitely come again. Fenrik popped his knot in and out of me, leaving me gasping with pleasure before he took his hair in my hand.

"Can I come inside you? Are you ready?" he groaned into my ear.

"Yes, yes," I panted, feeling another orgasm barreling down my spine at the sensation of his knot breaching me again and again.

Fenrik thrust once, twice more, before I felt his knot swell and thicken, unleashing rope after rope of cum into me. I came with him, a garbled mess of sensation, but could not be more pleased.

CHAPTER 13

FENRIK

*I*t wasn't even noon, and I had two fat haris. I was humming and heading back to our cabin when two orkin stepped out from the forest and onto the path before me. I recognized them as two members of our guard: Nils and Gris.

"Hello, Fenrik," Gris rasped in his low voice. "We've been looking for you for quite some time."

"Well, you can't have been looking very hard. I have been in the same place for almost a manathur," I sneered.

"Well, we've found you now, and you are returning with us. The jarl would like to speak with you." Nils grabbed my wrist while Gris pulled out a length of knotted rope.

"You mean to bring me back like a prisoner?" I knew the jarl wasn't happy that I didn't want to take his daughter as a mate, but I didn't think he was upset enough to take me captive.

"If that's what it takes." Gris tossed the haris aside as he bound my hands together. "Maybe we'll put in a good word for you if you don't fight us all the way back." He prodded me in the back with the butt of his spear to get me walking.

They marched me back to the tribe at a blistering pace, but I didn't fight or complain. My mind was working the entire time. I had to figure out how to get to Tracy. I'd told her I was going hunting, but she would start to panic when I didn't return. I only hoped she would listen to my warning and stay in the cabin. The thought of her wandering alone through the forest made me feel physically ill. If I ran for it now, I would be outnumbered. I hated to admit it, but together, Nils and Gris could take me down and tie me up completely, leaving me no choice but to return to the village —and they'd tell the jarl I'd fought them. It was in my best interest, and Tracy's, to go willingly.

The sun was low in the sky when we finally approached the village. I hadn't figured out what I would do about Tracy. Nils and Gris took me straight to the longhouse. The entire tribe was there for the last meal, and a silence fell over the room as Nils and Gris took me up to the head table. Jarl Gorm was seated, surrounded by the other elders, with Kelda to his left, and much to my surprise, she was holding hands with Sven, one of our older cooks. They appeared to be utterly smitten with each other.

As Gorm watched me approach, he placed his elbows on the table and pressed his fingers together, assessing me. "Well, they finally found you. It has been so long I thought you'd perished out in the forest."

My brain was working overtime, trying to figure out what Gorm was thinking. Would he punish me for fleeing and embarrassing his daughter? What is the worst he could do? Exile? That would be fine. I could go to Tracy, and we could even build a new home if we couldn't use the outpost anymore. That was probably the best-case scenario. Worst case? He could order me killed. Gorm was a fierce leader, but I doubted death was on the table. I shifted my weight from one foot to another as Gorm's eyes continued to bore into me.

Finally, I couldn't take it any longer. "Well, what are your plans for me? It doesn't seem as if taking Kelda as a mate is an option anymore."

Gorm's eyes flicked to his daughter. She wasn't even paying attention to our conversation.

"Luckily for you, once you *fled*," he spit out the word with venom, "Sven approached me. Apparently, he had always been interested in Kelda but thought I wouldn't consider him worthy as a mere kitchen worker. While Sven might not have been who I would have chosen, he and Kelda are very happy."

Hope bubbled up in my chest. "So it seems my decision not to take Kelda as my mate was for the best?"

Gorm scowled. "The fact that my daughter is now happily mated does not dissolve the need for some punishment for your failing to follow a direct order. You cannot be trusted as a hunter anymore. You will be stripped of your hunter status. You can either work in the kitchens or work in the fields. Your choice."

I tried to keep my face as neutral as possible, not wanting to give away my surprise at my punishment.

"I'll work the fields," I tried to say with a tone of disgust.

I was secretly elated. The tribe viewed farming and the kitchen as "soft" work, but it wouldn't bother me in the slightest. Not being able to leave the village would mean more time with Tracy—if I was somehow able to get the tribe to welcome her in. I would be home for her every night and could even have midday meals with her. Now I just had to get her here.

"Very well, you can start in the morning," Gorm said. "You look in dire need of a bath."

He sniffed the air as if he could smell me from across the table.

Fuck. I needed to get Tracy. "Um, may I be allowed to return to the outpost to collect some things?"

"What could you possibly have of value at the outpost?" he asked, glaring at me.

Throwing caution to the wind, I said, "Well, it isn't so much as some things as it is some*one*."

Silence hung thick in the air as Gorm studied me. "What do you mean someone?"

I quickly explained how Tracy arrived at the cabin and that she had been staying there since, having no place else to go. I referred to her as an alien—which she was—but I didn't want Gorm to get any ideas about how much she meant to me. He'd could easily come up with some sick way to use it against me.

When I finished the story, Gorm's disbelief was written all over his face, and his raised eyebrows were a clear sign. "You expect me to believe you have been living with a life-form from another planet since you ran?"

"Well, they didn't have anywhere else to go and had no idea how to care for themselves, so... yeah..." I finished lamely.

"I don't believe this nonsense. Gris! Nils! Get some food and then head to the outpost. Retrieve whatever or"—he gave me a withering stare—"whoever is there and return to the village."

I opened my mouth to protest. Tracy would be terrified of orkin strangers walking into our cabin.

"Jarl—" I began, but he cut me off.

"There is no way I am letting you leave again, Fenrik. I am not sure I even believe your story. It sounds like a fabrication to get away from the village again. Now go shower and get out of my sight." He waved me off with a disgusted noise.

I headed out of the longhouse, shoulders slumped in defeat. I was barely aware of my surroundings as I headed to the sauna. It was late, so I was the only one there. Distracted as I was by what would happen to Tracy, I couldn't deny it felt good to be properly clean for the first time in a long time. I showered and headed to my cabin. It was unusual for single males to have their own cabin, but I was older and had shown no sign of finding a mate, so the tribe let me build a small cabin for myself rather than living as a grown orc with my parents. I pushed open the door to find it completely untouched. Even my half-eaten meal was left from the night I fled.

I cleaned up the bare minimum and then headed to bed. My chest clenched, thinking about what Gris and Nils would do when they found Tracy. They wouldn't hurt her, Gorm would be furious, but they wouldn't coax her out like the delicate thing she was. She would be terrified.

I contemplated sneaking out to find her, but saw Gorm had placed two guards outside my door. Stupid bastard. I climbed back into bed and I lay there for a long time unable to get comfortable, and when I eventually fell asleep, I drifted in and out of nightmares of Tracy screaming and her blue eyes wide with terror. No matter how hard I tried I couldn't get to her.

TRACY

Fenrik had left early the next morning, we were low on meat. I decided to bathe and wash the bedding. We both needed it —and it would keep my mind off of Fenrik out in the woods alone. I trudged outside, washing supplies thrown in a basket. It wasn't so much that it was heavy, as it was awkward to carry down to the stream.

By the time I finished washing and hanging up the bedding, it was nearly midday, and he hadn't come back, but that wasn't abnormal. I ate some of our remaining dried meat and tidied while waiting for him to return.

I started to worry as the sun began to sink. I rushed and pulled the sun-warmed bedding off the line before the sun set completely. Not sure what else to do with myself, I made the bed. Then, with the last rays of the sun, I built a fire in the bedroom fireplace. I didn't have the energy to build one in the living room—it wasn't like anyone was sitting there, anyway. The sun had completely set, and it was a moonless night. I stood at the bedroom window for a long time wishing Fenrik would appear, before I gave up and sat at the edge of *our* bed.

I tried not to dwell on what might have happened. Fenrik would never leave me. He must have gotten hurt. The idea was almost more than I could handle, and I felt my chest grow tight at the thought of him alone and injured out in the forest's darkness.

No, he had to be fine. He was probably just caught up in hunting. He was very capable, even at night. Orcs had much better vision than humans. I'd learned when we'd gone on walks that he tried to point out flora and fauna to me, and I was insistent he was imagining things.

Fenrik was fine, just struggling to find food. I told myself this repeatedly as I curled into a ball on the bed. He'd be here when I woke up. He'd snuggle up to me and spoon me until I awoke. Fenrik was fine. He had to be fine.

I was jolted awake by a large bang in the living room. Something—or someone—had hit the cabin enough to cause it to shake. I sat up in the bed, torn between hiding in the bedroom and running to see what had caused the commotion. I wasn't going to be one of those dumb white girls in horror movies that ran toward danger. The bedroom window was big enough for me to fit out of, and I was considering if I was strong enough to push it open when the bedroom door was flung open with such force that it bounced off the wall. On the other side of the door stood two hulking orcs, neither of which were Fenrik. I tried to scream, but it was lodged in my throat as the two orcs looked at me intently.

"That's it," the shorter one said, cocking his head to the side and squinting as if his vision wasn't the best.

"Já, yellow hair," the taller, scarier-looking one rasped.

He had a scar that bisected his face, running from his jaw to his temple, and he looked at me with such ferocity that I felt myself start to tremble. Whoever they were, they were here for me. I stepped toward the window, but the taller one was fast. He wrapped his arms around my waist before I had made it two steps. I struggled, kicked, and clawed, but I might as well have been fighting a boulder because of his strength. He was even taller than Fenrik and just as muscular. Finally finding my voice, I started screaming my head off while trying to free myself from this massive, grouchy orc's grip.

The shorter one covered his pointed ears. "Can you get it to stop making so much noise?"

"I don't know why it is screaming," the grouchy one rasped.

They were referring to me as "it" as if I wasn't sentient,

and with every kick and scream, Mr. Grouchy's hold on me got even tighter until it felt like he was crushing me. My panic went from high to off-the-charts as I started to feel like I couldn't breathe. I struggled and struggled until I felt my vision start to tunnel. My breath was coming in short, shallow bursts, and I knew what was coming as I continued to claw against my captor, but it was too late. I was going under. My vision winked out. My last thought was *I can't be abducted again.*

CHAPTER 14

TRACY

$\mathcal{I}$ woke up to the sunlight coming through a
window. I stayed absolutely still as I tried to figure
out where I was. The cabin looked similar to the one I had
been staying in with Fenrik, but it was one room with several
low cots and a long workbench along one wall. I seemed to
be completely alone. I held my breath, ready for some other
attack, based on what had already happened.

The two hulking orcs that had taken me didn't really
harm me, but they'd abducted me, nonetheless. I had no idea
where I was and, worse, I wasn't with Fenrik.

I started to spiral. I'd just lost my only rock on this alien
planet. Not only was he my island in the middle of the sea,
but I was pretty sure I loved him. I had to find him.

I started to sit up when I heard steps approaching. I
quickly lay back down and pretended to be asleep. I could
hear whoever it was walking around the cabin muttering.
Based on their voice, they seemed to be female.

I squinted my eyes open the tiniest sliver. An elderly female orc was puttering around by the workbench. I could only see her profile, but her black hair was streaked liberally with gray, and I could make out the wrinkles on her face as she frowned at whatever she was working with. I raised my head slightly in an attempt to see more, still not wanting her to realize I was awake. Without warning, she turned to me with a mug in hand. She'd caught me watching her.

To my surprise, she beamed at me. "You're awake!"

"Yes, I think?" I scrunched my face up in confusion. Whatever was happening, I didn't seem to be in a hostile situation. "Where am I?"

"You're in the healer's cabin at Snaerfire. And I'm the healer, Thyra." She offered me the mug.

I sat up and took it, sniffing it suspiciously. "What is this?"

"It's healing tea. I have already bandaged your cuts and scrapes, which should aid your recovery. It also has a calming effect, which it looks like you might need."

My brain whirred as I sipped the tea. "Is Fenrik here?"

"Yes, but it is still early, and I doubt he is awake yet. After his ordeal yesterday, he could use the rest. We'll let him know you got here…somewhat safely… thanks to Gris and Nils." She rolled her eyes.

I was alarmed. "What do you mean, his ordeal?"

"The tribe has been looking for him for over a manathur. Gris and Nils found him last night and marched him back to the village. Gorm stripped him of his role as a hunter in front of the entire tribe," she said mournfully.

She seemed truly upset about Fenrik's fate.

"What will he do instead?"

"He agreed to farm the fields."

"What's wrong with farming?" I asked, confused. *Farmers seemed like solid people back on Earth.*

"Nothing, nothing. But he always dreamed of being a

hunter like his dad. He'll make a fine farmer. I worry whether or not he'll be happy." Her eyes looked misty.

I wondered how well she knew Fenrik, given her level of concern for his future. I needed to know what was going on.

"Can I go see him? Right now?" I tried to keep the panic out of my voice.

"Of course, dear. Do you think you can walk?" She offered me her arm, and we headed out of the cabin.

I was in nothing but one of Fenrik's tunics, but it hung down to almost my knees. I was too focused on getting to him to even care. We walked a way along a cobblestone path until it split off, one way continuing with the cobblestone and the other a well-worn tree-lined path. It felt as if we were heading out of the village.

As if sensing my unspoken question, the orc woman said, "Fenrik decided he wanted to be a little out of the village when he built his cabin, he likes his peace. I think that's another reason he wanted to be a hunter."

We approached the front door of a small but tidy-looking cabin with a wrap-around porch, and Thyra opened it without knocking.

"Fenrik!" she called as we stood in the doorway. "I've brought you Tracy!"

Grumbling came from the adjacent room almost immediately, and the door opened to reveal a shirtless Fenrik. Without a thought, I ran and flung myself around him, arms and legs wrapping his body tightly. I didn't care who Thyra was or that she was watching. For too long, I'd been without Fenrik, my rock, the only soul I knew on this wild planet. I had spent so many hours wondering if he was hurt or lost that seeing him in the flesh had me burying my face into his neck, clutching him tightly. His big arms enveloped me, pulling me even closer to him, our bodies pressed against each other.

I felt him take a deep breath, breathing in my scent, holding me tightly.

"I've got her, Ma—I will formally introduce you later," Fenrik called to Thyra before taking me back to the bedroom.

I heard Thyra quietly shut the bedroom door, no questions asked. I tried to stop the tears from leaking all over Fenrik's neck while also trying to make sense of what I'd just heard.

"Is Thyra… your mom?"

"Yes. She's the reason I knew to get you on herbs for birth control. She is the tribe's herbalist and healer."

"And…" I paused, unsure what to say. "And… does she know about me?"

"Well, the fact that she delivered you to me and watched you jump into my arms would suggest she has an idea," he murmured into my hair as he carried me into his room.

It was adorned in blues and greens, and I wanted to sink into the giant bed immediately. Fenrik sat me down on the edge of it, his eyes never leaving me. He traced his fingers over my skin, seeing some bruises and marks.

"Did Gris and Nils do this to you?" he growled.

"Well, yes. Two unfamiliar orcs barged into our cabin and essentially said 'this is the one we want.' I wasn't going down without a fight. I screamed and kicked and clawed at them as they tried to take me. I think I might have actually bitten one of them." I grimaced. "If they had just *told me* they were taking me to you, I would have gone willingly."

Fenrik pursed his lips in disbelief.

"Well. Probably not willingly, but I would have at least known that they were from your tribe and might not have fought so hard."

I didn't think it was possible, but Fenrik raised his brows even further. They threatened to disappear into his hairline.

"For some reason I don't think that would have been enough to convince you to go quietly."

"Well…" I trailed off.

He was probably right.

"But Fenrik, you haven't told me how you ended up back in your village. You didn't leave willingly… did you?" I asked.

Fenrik's face softened immediately as he scooted off the edge of the bed and knelt in front of me. Cupping my face in his giant hands he brushed his lips across mine.

"Never," he said fiercely. "I would never leave you. You are my everything. Nils and Gris found me first and informed me I was being taken back to the tribe in no uncertain terms. I was outnumbered and caught completely by surprise. I let them lead me back here, but my thoughts never strayed from how you would panic when I didn't return. As soon as they brought me to Gorm, I requested to return for you."

"And he didn't trust you to leave and return? Thyra—your mom—said he stripped you of your title as hunter. Is that serious?"

"No. He said I was to stay in my cabin with guards posted outside. It was only once Ma threw a fit, insisting I wouldn't go anywhere without you that he had them removed this morning. She's got an exceptional sway with him, being the only healer. I tossed and turned all night, worried what they would do to you." He paused, taking a long breath. "And yes, Gorm stripped me of my position as hunter. It is a position of prestige in our tribe. I am now Farmer Fenrik." He gave me a lopsided smile.

I got the feeling he wasn't telling me the whole truth. "Do you want to be a farmer?"

"Well, not really. At least I didn't want to before. I like being out on my own. I didn't have anyone at the tribe to come home to, so staying out hunting for nights on end never bothered me. It gave me my space and made me a useful member of the tribe. But now..." he trailed off, hanging his head.

"What aren't you telling me?" I pressed. Silence hung in the air for a moment.

He sighed. "I could be a farmer. I would be, happily—if it meant I had you at my side."

He said it all so quietly it was barely a whisper, as if he spoke it out loud, it would be taken from him.

"Fenrik." I pulled his chin up so we were eye to eye. "I would *love* to farm alongside you."

"Really? You'd stay? After how they've treated you?"

I pretended to think about it for a moment, tapping my chin with my finger. "Nils and Gris aren't farmers are they?" I asked with a grin.

"No." He smiled. "No, they are guards."

"Well then, sign me up for a life of farming!" I threw my arms around his neck and pulled him to me. I kissed him with everything I had, then whispered into his lips as I slid my fingers through his hair, "I will farm for the rest of my days if I get to do it by your side."

"You're sure? It's not a very exciting life."

"Who said I wanted exciting? I think I have had plenty of excitement in the past few weeks. Settling down with you sounds like a dream."

"We're going to have to work some things out. Gorm didn't even want to let Nils and Gris get you. At first, he said to leave you out to die. Gorm thought he could punish me by not letting me get you. Even though I am grateful he decided to go get you, Gorm hasn't given any indication that he'll allow you to stay. If he doesn't... I am not sure what we can do. But I wouldn't let you leave without me. We'll speak to Gorm today."

"Do you have any idea of what he is thinking?" This was a

new worry I hadn't considered. If they didn't let me stay, where would I go?

"Gorm doesn't like outsiders and he's definitely not a fan of me. But we've never had someone be dropped from the sky before, so I don't know. I think if anyone has pull it will be my mom."

While I appreciated Fenrik was being honest with me about our options, it wasn't doing anything to soothe my nerves.

"Hey." He grabbed my face with both his hands so I'd have to look him in the eye. "I'm here now. We're here together. Even if we can't stay here, I am not leaving you. I've run once before." He took me back to his bed, laying me down, and began to kiss up and down my neck before attacking my lips with fervor. "I want you forever," he said between kisses.

CHAPTER 15

$\mathcal{M}$y Tracy, back in my arms. My hands bracketed her as I swooped down to devour her lips. She was relatively unharmed, aside from the cuts and bruises she obtained trying to fight off Nils and Gris. I continued to kiss her before pulling back to check in with her.

"Is this what you want to do right now?" I asked her, uncertain.

"This is exactly what I want to do right now," she said, wrapping her legs around my hips and pulling me closer.

There would be so much to figure out, including how Tracy would react to the tribe and whether the tribe would accept her, but I would be with her here and now. I stroked her hair and slid my fingers along her jaw, admiring her bright blue eyes that never left my face.

She pulled me in for another kiss, settling my hips into hers. I wanted to touch her everywhere. We continued to kiss as I dipped my fingers under her tunic, slowly drawing it up. Tracy drew her hands up over her head, and I pulled her tunic off her, leaving her lips for only a moment. With her tunic gone, her bare chest was against mine. I slid my tongue into her mouth, dragging it along hers. It was amazing and unreal to have Tracy here in my bed. We'd spent so much time just getting by and trying to stay alive out in the woods. Having her somewhere with all the comforts of home was ecstasy. I groaned as she pulled me even closer as if trying to merge with me.

Tracy pressed her hand between our bodies, sliding it down my stomach and attempting to unlace my leather pants. Without pulling my lips from hers, I reached down to help, desperate to be inside her. Now that I knew she was okay and here—with me—I was ravenous for her.

We quickly unlaced and pulled my pants down together and, within seconds, we were both naked and pressed against each other desperately. I flipped us so Tracy was on top of me, wanting to see all of her. I scanned down her perfect form. Her cheeks were flushed, and her parted lips were swollen and red from our kissing. My eyes traveled down to her breasts, and her nipples hardened with want.

I couldn't stop myself. I raised my hands and teased each nipple, causing her to arch into my touch. I pinched them before dragging my thumb over each and shifting up on my elbows to bring one peaked nipple into my mouth. I flicked my tongue over it before suctioning down on her entire breast as if to draw milk from it. In the time I had been with Tracy, I learned that there was nothing like sucking on her nipples to get her wet and ready for me.

She moaned and ground her hips into mine, sliding my cock up and down her folds. I wrapped my hands around her hips easily and lifted her up so I could slide home into her warm heat. We moaned in unison. This was a dance we'd now done many times, but I never tired of it. I loved when Tracy rode me, her breasts bouncing with every thrust and mouth thrown open in ecstasy.

Though we hadn't been apart for long, neither of us were going to last long, given the joy and relief we both felt at finding each other alive and whole. I watched where our bodies were connected. I dragged my fingers across each of Tracy's nipples before trailing my fingers down to her lower lips, finding her hidden button right at the top. It only took a few quick circles with my thumb before I felt her clamping down on me and falling forward as I unleashed inside her, unable to keep the quiet growl of "mine" from escaping my throat.

TRACY

I lay spread out, fucked boneless, as Fenrik got up.

"I'll get some towels to clean us up." He bent over and kissed my forehead before heading out of the bedroom.

As I admired his taut ass, I noticed a marking on his back I had never seen before. Down the length of his spine was a tattoo that looked like the ocean's waves. It traveled from the nape of his neck down to his pelvis. *Surely I would have noticed a tattoo like this before?*

"Uh, did Gorm give you a tattoo as punishment?" I asked.

"Hmm?"

"You have a tattoo down your back that I have never seen before."

Fenrik rushed out of the room without explanation. I stood, dripping with his cum, and followed him. He headed to a small washroom with only a sink and a toilet. I watched as he turned and tried to see the markings. He grabbed me by the shoulders and spun me.

"Oh gods—I never expected—I assumed it wasn't possible," he stuttered.

"What? What is happening?" I was utterly perplexed and annoyed at being left in the dark.

Fenrik spun me around. "Look at your back."

I gasped to see a marking down my spine that matched his identically. "What is this?"

"It's our mate markings. We are mates." He pulled me into a crushing embrace.

"Mates?" I asked, confused. "What does that even mean?"

"It means we are fated to be together," Fenrik explained, pulling me even tighter against his chest.

I froze.

"You don't have fated mates on Earth, right?" Fenrik asked, gently pulling away

"No. We have marriage and divorce. We talked about this," I said, suddenly feeling shivers all over. "You said mates are forever, right?"

"Mates are for life. Usually, when one dies, the other goes shortly after. They are your one true match."

"And what if a few years into your… matehood, you don't get along anymore? And you want out?" I asked. I went into my marriage unhappy, but I had plenty of friends that had started theirs expecting it to be wonderful only to find themselves miserable a few years in. *What if that happened to us?*

"I have never known that to happen, but I have known orkin to reject the matebond. If you reject the matebond, your marks fade over time. You can take another *chosen* mate but never get another Elska mate."

"So, it's you or… maybe someone else? Maybe no one?" I asked bluntly. I didn't like that option either. I didn't want anyone else, but I also didn't want to be *alone* on an alien planet for the rest of my days.

"Well," he hesitated. "Yes? That is how it works with fated mates."

"How long do I have to decide?" I crossed my arms in front of myself, looking around the room. I would do anything to meet Fenrik's gaze. He seemed elated.

"I don't know. I don't know anyone who has not decided," he said quietly. "It is always accepted." I could tell though that my uncertainty was hurting him.

"I can't, Fenrik. I just can't. You know what it was like with Gabe. I had no choice. I need to have at least have a minute to wrap my mind around it. Even though every fiber of my being is telling me to hurl myself at you, I need some time to think." I tapped my fingers across my lips. "I've been in a cult before, and it was not a good time. Have some unknown fate decide my partner for life is a lot. Though… I guess it's better than your parents choosing."

Anything had to be better than your parents choosing. *Right?*

"I understand." He nodded, but it clearly made him sad. "Do you want me to go and give you space to think?"

"Can't I decide with you here?" I asked, unable to keep the quaver out of my voice. Fenrik was my rock. How was I supposed to make a decision like this without him?

Fenrik looked confused. "You want to make a decision as to whether or not we are mates with me still here?"

"Well, can't it be a decision we make together?" I asked, well aware of how forlorn I sounded.

Fenrik slumped over in relief. "Of course, we can make the decision together."

"I wouldn't want to make it without you," I said, rolling it over more carefully in my head. *Why wouldn't a couple want to decide this together? That seems dumb.* "This involves both our futures."

Fenrik looked surprised but pleased. "So you want to stay in my cabin and decide if we should be mated?"

"That's exactly what I want to do." I pulled him in for a kiss.

"Well, I don't think Elska mates have ever happened this way, but I am happy to do whatever makes you comfortable." He nuzzled into my neck.

❧

The next morning, as I lay awake with Fenrik, who was still asleep with an arm strewn across my stomach, thinking about the night before. I had to acknowledge that some of my resistance to having a "fated mate" came from feeling trapped my whole life. At first glance this looked like another trap. But this *was* different. Fenrik would let me walk away if I wanted to. He'd reiterated it multiple times. Even though I could tell he was clearly distressed at the idea of me leaving, he would let me—if it was what *I* wanted. That was a cataclysmic shift from my old life. Maybe this is why we were fated in the first place. The universe knew I needed someone who would give me the freedom to decide.

Fenrik was clearly used to his privacy—living slightly removed from the town. I could happily assimilate into that. Living on the edge of the village would provide me with the sanctuary I needed. After growing up in a cult, someone who enjoyed privacy was a breath of fresh air. Fenrik had become my everything in our month together—my North Star that I had never found on Earth. This wasn't the same as being forced into something. While I had my fears, Fenrik had made it clear I'd be able to be my own person—if the tribe would have me. He'd proven time and time again that he would put my needs first, tribe or not. I dragged my finger's across his chest to wake him.

Without a word, he pulled me to his chest, nuzzling his nose into my hair.

"Good morning," he murmured.

We stayed wrapped together for a while, and I voiced a question that I was worried to bring up.

"Will they accept me?" I asked, even though we'd talked about it the previous night.

"I don't know. But if they don't, I am going with you," he responded without hesitation.

"And if they let us stay, we can still be together, on the edge of the tribe?" I hesitated.

"If that is what you want, we can remain isolated, only participating in tribal activities when we feel inclined to do so." Fenrik said.

I tried to let my brain wrap around that for a moment. Where I was from, *everything* was an obligation. It was hard for me to imagine skipping community events simply for my own comfort. *To not go to a potluck because I don't feel like it? Sacrilege.*

"Do you like participating in tribal events?" I asked quietly.

"Some of them. The winter solstice is nice. But I don't go to many of them." He paused. "Being a hunter, that was an option for me. I am unsure how that will change now that I am a farmer."

"So what now?" I asked meekly.

"Well, we will have to present you to the tribe." Fenrik stroked my cheek as I blanched. "Shh, it will be fine. I am sure my mother will already have alerted the jarl to the situation. And once everyone finds out about our matebond, it will likely make it very difficult for them to send you away. The matebond is respected above all else here."

"Do you think I could meet just a few of them at a time?" I chewed my lip.

"Why don't you go take a bath? I will get us some breakfast and fresh clothes, and then I will have a few elders come meet you." Fenrik disentangled himself from me, leaving me with warm cum dripping out of me.

"A *few* elders?" I squinted at him.

"No more than four. Promise." He kissed me on the forehead and headed to the washroom to clean up. "Take a bath, relax. Gathering everyone and getting you some food will take me some time."

I wrapped myself in a blanket and headed to the bathroom, where the sunken tub was still slightly steaming as if calling me to get in. I quickly disrobed and gingerly stepped into the water, sinking in until I could lie back against one of the sides, with the water up to my neck. I had bathed more times in the last two days than I had in a month. It was more like a jacuzzi than a bathtub, but that made sense if it was designed to fit an orc.

I relaxed for a long time, unpacking the events from the last few days. I was strangely calm about the whole mate thing. It isn't as if I'd had a choice with Gabe. At least with Fenrik, there was an out if I wanted one that didn't involve sneaking out in the middle of the night and taking a bus to some unknown town.

I would miss the beach, though. I loved the sound of the

waves lapping on the shore, lulling me to sleep at night. But there had been a long, glorious line of sand, oceans that went on for what felt like an eternity and somehow made me feel more infinite than any church sermon ever did. I sighed, burying my head in my hands. If I was trapped on an alien planet forever, the thing I would miss most was the beach. I wondered briefly if they had beaches here, or if it was all rivers and creepy double-toothed bears.

Eventually, I started to get pruny, so I carefully scrubbed myself all over before washing my hair. I was wrapping myself in one of the fluffy towels when I heard the front door open. I poked my head out, relieved to see only Fenrik carrying a tray of what looked like croissants and a bag over his shoulder. He set down the food and, without skipping a beat, scooped me up and carried me bridal-style back to the bedroom. I giggled as he flopped me onto his bed and removed the bag he was wearing. He handed it to me.

"I hope you find something you like in there." His eyes roved me hungrily as my towel unwound, exposing my breasts. "Though, if it weren't for the elders arriving shortly, I would keep you as is."

"Shortly?" I yelped, grabbing the bag. "How shortly?"

"I asked them to give us time to have breakfast and get dressed."

I opened the bag and pulled out a tunic and pants. The tunic even had pretty embroidery stitched around the collar and the sleeves. It was loose on me and the pants were a bit long, but I was used to that by now.

"I tried to get some hand-me-downs from an orc female that has not yet come of age," Fenrik said, "figuring they'd fit better."

I looked in the bag to find that the tunic had a pretty embroidered belt. Tying it around my waist, I felt more put together than I had since I'd arrived on this planet in my skimpy pink dress. My stomach growled, causing Fenrik to steer me toward the kitchen. We were sitting down to eat when a knock came at the door.

CHAPTER 16

FENRIK

I opened my front door, ushering in Gorm, Lilja, Katla, and my mom. I'd worked hard to convince Gorm to meet with us—especially in the privacy of my home. I was pretty certain that Kelda and my mom had something to do with his final agreement.

"Tracy, this is Jarl Gorm, Lilja, the farming elder. Katla, the elder of the kitchens, and you've met my mom, the tribe's healer," I explained as I indicated each of them in turn. "Everyone, this is Tracy."

Tracy's blue eyes were wide as she hastily tried to finish her mouthful of pastry with an audible swallow.

"Why don't we all sit?" I pointed to my living area, which had a sofa and chairs. Tracy sat on the couch beside me, tightly wrapping her tiny hand around mine.

Gorm studied Tracy curiously. "What are you?" he asked after a time.

I sighed. I had already explained Tracy's entire abduction

story and where she came from so that she wouldn't have to go through this whole ordeal.

"I—I'm a human from Earth," she stammered.

"And you were dropped here by some other creatures—"

I cut him off angrily. "Gorm, I have already explained all of this to you. You know how she arrived here and feels safe with me. I don't think she is ready to trust others just yet. Especially not after the treatment Nils and Gris gave her." I gave him a look filled with scorn.

"So then, what are your intentions with her? Are you keeping her as a pet?"

"Of course he doesn't want to keep her as a pet, you idiot," my mom interjected. "Open your eyes."

It was only my mother's high station as healer that enabled her to get away with talking to Gorm with such disrespect. Though his treatment of me and Tracy still left plenty of room for improvement, the bare level of decency we were receiving had to be down to Ma.

Gorm seemed to register for the first time that Tracy's body pressed against mine, our hands wrapped together. His brows raised.

"You mean to take her as a mate?" he asked. "But she's so small. How do you know if you..." He coughed uncomfortably and trailed off.

I laughed to myself quietly. He wanted to ask how she and I fit but didn't want to say it outright.

I stood, Tracy still clinging to my hand. I turned so my back was to Gorm and the others and raised my tunic. I heard a collective gasp.

"Elskas," whispered Lilja.

"Fenrik! Why didn't you tell me she was your Elska?!" Ma demanded immediately.

"I wasn't keeping it from you. I just needed to get her

settled before we figured out what to do next," I said as an apology.

"How do we know it's her and not another female?" Gorm asked, unconvinced.

To my surprise, Tracy stood quickly and pulled up the back of her own tunic, revealing her matching marks—which received another collective gasp. Tracy turned and faced Gorm, crossing her arms over her chest and giving him a look that clearly said *I told you so.* Gorm's jaw dropped. I covered my mouth to hide my laughter, but I loved when Tracy's sass came out. I took a deep breath before continuing.

"So you see, whatever your ridiculous plans were for us, you can't really separate Elska mates."

It was almost as if I could see the cogs in Gorm's brain working as Mom rushed up and hugged Tracy tightly.

"I'd always hoped Fenrik would settle down, but he's such the solitary type, I'd given up." Her eyes glistened as she continued to hug a very alarmed Tracy, who had her arms trapped to her sides due to the embrace.

"Ma, Ma, let her go. This is all new for her." Mom released her, and I stepped in, putting myself between them.

"Excuse me," Tracy finally spoke. "Can we stop talking about me as if I am not here? I want to be part of the decision about what happens to me. Especially as to whether or not Fenrik can *keep* me." She gave Gorm a withering look.

He had the decency to look ashamed of himself.

"Of course, of course, dear. Do you want to stay with Fenrik? He has explained that you can reject the bond, right?" Mom placed her hand gently on Tracy's arm.

Tracy nodded. "Yes, he told me I could reject him as a mate… but if *permitted*"—she gave Gorm an icy stare—"I'd like to stay with him."

"Trace, you don't have to commit—"

"I know I don't have to," she said. "I am choosing to." Tracy grabbed my hand. She was resolute.

"Are you sure?"

"I told you I wasn't ready to be part of a tight-knit community again, but this? Here? I can do this. I can live on the edge of the village with you." She squeezed my hand.

"You don't have the right—" Gorm started but was met with death glares by the three female elders.

"The right to what, exactly?" Katla asked coolly.

Gorm put his hands up in defeat. "Fine. Let him keep his human. But he is still stripped of his hunting rights. I don't need him going off and one of us having to care for his... mate," he spat the word out.

I stepped to him, ready to swing, but Mom blocked my path. "She will have a place here as his Elska," she said with gritted teeth. "This should be for celebration as we have not had a new matebond form in quite some time."

"And what will she do while she's here to earn her keep?" Gorm asked petulantly

"I'd like to stay with Fenrik for now, so if he's farming, then I am farming," Tracy said more firmly than I expected. "I had to grow a small vegetable and herb garden back... home. I am sure I can be of use when it comes to farming."

I wanted to grab Tracy off the ground and spin her around. I was so happy that not only did she want to stay, but she also wanted to be with me as I worked. However, I held myself back, as the elders were still in my living room.

"Fine." Gorm gave a jerk of his head and walked out.

Katla and Lilja stayed only long enough to welcome Tracy a bit more warmly and then followed Gorm out, leaving me with just Mom and Tracy. Mom's eyes still shined brightly as she held back tears.

"I know you two won't want a big party celebrating your bond," Mom said, hesitating, "but what about a small dinner with some of your closest friends? So that Tracy can get to know a few friendly faces?" She looked at both of us hopefully.

Tracy squeezed my hand before responding, "That sounds lovely, thank you."

I could tell Mom wanted to hug Tracy again, but she settled on hugging me, giving Tracy a small wave, and letting herself out. Finally, Tracy and I were alone.

We headed to the couch, and I pulled Tracy into my lap. I nuzzled my nose into her long, wavy locks, breathing in her scent.

"Are you sure about all this?" I pulled back to look her in the eye. "You didn't have to say yes just because they were all here. I don't want you to stay unless it is what you really want. I'd take you to another tribe to see if you liked it there... I'm sorry I don't have a way to take you home."

Tracy smiled and stroked her fingers up my arm before cupping my face with her tiny hands. "You are exactly what I want. And if I have to learn how to grow alien vegetables to be with you, I will do it—but no big welcome party."

"Right, there will be no welcome party. Just dinner with my mom and a few close friends," I assured her. "You can meet the rest of the tribe at your own pace."

"Do you want to get back to our breakfast?" I gestured to the half-eaten pastries still on the table.

As if suddenly remembering she was still hungry, Tracy hopped off my lap and returned to her breakfast.

"So small dinner with your mom tonight. What's in store for the day?" she asked through a mouthful of food.

"Maybe we could introduce you to the other farmers?"

"How many of them are there?"

"Three."

"Oh." She looked relieved. "I can handle three."

TRACY

Fenrik and I walked hand in hand around the edge of the tribe to the farm area. He assured me we were unlikely to meet anyone as it was the middle of the day. It wasn't that I was *afraid* of meeting his tribe. I just needed to do it in small chunks. And I would need to be constantly reassured that I could live the life I wanted here—not a life prescribed for me. Meeting the other farmers I would work with seemed like a good starting place. I didn't mind the idea of farming. It sounded better than keeping house for Gabe and cooking all his meals, and I loved being outside.

It wasn't long before we reached the farmlands. They weren't particularly large, but everything was growing in neat rows—some vegetables that looked sort of familiar and some that were utterly alien to me. As we approached, an orc female was tending to a plant that was growing what looked like a cross between a tomato and a bell pepper. She waved us over. I followed Fenrik's lead, and we joined her among the plants.

"So, are you ready for farm life?" She arched a brow at Fenrik.

Fenrick cleared his throat. "Well, some things have changed since I left the tribe. Let's just say I would rather not go off on long hunting trips anymore." He inclined his head toward me.

She gave me a wide smile. "Thyra has told me all about you. It's a pleasure to meet you, Tracy. My name is Greta."

"Hello, nice to meet you too," I said, trying not to sound too timid.

"Well, let me show you around, and we can figure out where you are best suited."

We wandered through the rows and rows of plants, with Greta telling me the names and seasons of each one until I felt like my head was swimming with information. She was explaining how to keep mold off of a radish-type plant when a young orc came running up to her.

"Ma, one of the chooklings has gone missing again," she wailed.

"Oh honey, they always come back, don't worry. They know who feeds them." She stroked the young girl's hair.

It was hard to tell the age of an entirely different species, but if I had to guess, she was about to enter her teen years. She was clearly distraught about the missing *chookling*, whatever that was. Something about her face screwed up, fighting off tears, pulled me to her.

"I can help look for the chookling," I volunteered, secretly hoping a chookling was a small animal and not a large one.

The young orc looked at me, relief etched on her face. "You'll help?"

"Sure, if your mom is okay with it."

Greta nodded. The young orc grabbed my hand and we were off, weaving through the rows of plants to a small hut. *Okay, good. All signs pointing toward a small animal.*

"Biddy is missing. We have fourteen chooklings that I am in charge of, and Biddy is always the one that wanders off. I think she likes hunting for worms."

"Mmm, before we go hunting for Biddy, can you tell me what a chookling looks like—and maybe your name?"

"Oh." She blushed. "I'm Elin."

"Hi Elin, I'm Tracy."

Elin smiled at me and ducked into the little hut before returning with a chookling in her arms. I laughed out loud. A *chookling* was a chicken—well, mainly a chicken. Instead of feathers it had fur that looked incredibly soft, like a rabbit's. Its wings were tucked tight to its body, making me think chooklings probably didn't fly. But its face was almost exactly the same as an Earth chicken—slightly different eyes. Of course, I could help find a chicken.

Elin looked embarrassed. "What's so funny?"

"I just—" I tried to stop myself from laughing. "I was expecting some alien creature, and it's almost exactly like an animal we have back home, called a chicken. I know all about them."

"Oooh, do you want to help me with the chooklings? Sometimes I can get behind on gathering the eggs and everyone in the tribe depends on them."

"Sure, if your mom is okay with it, I can help you with the chooklings."

Elin beamed at me and dragged me back to her mom and Fenrik. Apparently, I was now to be a *chookling* farmer. I couldn't think of anything better.

CHAPTER 17

enrik and I fell into a routine. I would arrive at the farm early in the morning to help Elin collect the eggs from the chooklings and deliver them to the kitchen. Then Fenrik would meet me at the longhouse for breakfast before we'd head back to tending the village's farm. With the extra sets of hands Fenrik and I provided, the work wasn't taxing, and we were free most days by midafternoon. Fenrik and I would take long walks, and he'd point out all the different medicinal plants his mom used.

Before I knew it, two months had passed. Fenrik and I had been with his tribe longer than at the isolated cabin. True to his word, we mainly kept to ourselves, but I had met all the tribe members and liked them well enough. Fenrik had a small group of friends we would have over for dinner every few weeks. I'd formed a special bond with Elin and enjoyed spending my days caring for the chooklings with her. She, her mom, and her dad ran the farm, and they often had us over for meals. I couldn't ask for a more perfect balance of having a community without feeling like I was constantly being watched. It was as if fate plucked me up and dropped me exactly where I needed to be.

Fenrik and I were on one of our late afternoon walks, meandering through the trees and talking about our day, just enjoying each other's company in a way that still felt new. It was such a nice afternoon, and I was feeling so warm and gushy that this was how my life turned out. I had to stop Fenrik and pull him in for a kiss. I kissed him deeply, pulling on the collar of his tunic. When I released him, he had a surprised, but pleased look on his face.

"What was that for?" he asked, his interest clearly piqued.

"Because I love you. And I'm happy here. I can't believe I get to spend my days walking in the woods with you instead of cooking casseroles for Gabe and attending church potlucks I loathed."

"I love you too." He swooped down and took my lips with his, teasing them apart with his tongue. I groaned as his tongue tangled with mine, wrapping my arms around his neck. We continued to devour each other until I knew there was no turning back.

Fenrik grabbed my breast with one hand, using his other to squeeze the swell of my ass. I could feel his thickened cock as he ground into me.

"Should we head home—very quickly?" I gasped.

"No time for that." Fenrik started unlacing my pants.

"Fenrik! Out here!? In the open?" I whispered as if suddenly the bushes might be alive with orkin.

"Yes, here." His voice dipped low, but his hands still focused on removing my pants. "No one enjoys wandering the woods like you do. We will be fine."

He finished my laces and dipped his hand inside, his calloused fingers searching for the right spot. I panted and leaned my head against his chest as against his fingers glided across my already wet folds. He stroked me like that again and again until I was whining for more.

He chuckled. "I thought you were worried about getting caught."

"I don't give a fuck. I need you inside me. Now. Right now."

It was my turn to attack his pants. They were stretched taut over his growing bulge. I palmed it, relishing its weight before returning to the laces. It wasn't long before his cock sprang out, already solid and leaking from the tip. I stroked him while he continued to finger me, spreading my folds and gently flicking his thumb over my clit. I keened under him at the onslaught of sensations, pulling my lips from his briefly to ask, "Where?"

Fenrik's eyes whipped around the forest, looking for a good place, before spotting a boulder *just* the right height a little ways away. He removed his hand from my pants and hoisted me up over his shoulder, cock still proudly jutting out.

"Fenrik, I can walk!" I tried to hang on as he jostled me, walking quickly to the boulder.

"This is quicker," he growled.

I felt myself get even wetter. I loved it when the urgent, demanding side of Fenrik came out. He placed me down in front of the boulder before spinning me so my back was to him and I was bent over the bolder. He yanked down my pants and massaged the globes of my ass, and his hot breath tickled my neck.. He pressed kisses down my neck and across my shoulders. I whined in frustration. I wanted him.

"Stop teasing me," I begged.

"Oh, is there something you wanted?" Fenrik teased as he dipped two large fingers into my pussy, causing me to cry out.

He breached me slowly, testing if I was wet enough to take him. Even after being together for months and having sex ridiculously often, he still had to ready me for his size. Not that I minded. He pulled his fingers out, and I was frustrated that he stopped when I felt his broad cockhead slide up and down my folds, smearing his precum everywhere before finally slowly pushing into me. With my pants barely past my hips, I couldn't spread my legs very wide, making for an even tighter fit than usual. I reveled in feeling every ridge and textured braid of his cock as he invaded me. He could only fit up to his knot before sliding back out and thrusting again.

"Oh fuck, Trace, you feel so good like this, I don't think I can hold back," he groaned.

"Then don't."

A feral growl escaped him as he picked up the pace, hammering in and out of me, lighting me on fire from the inside out. The flame grew and grew as I hurtled towards my peak, but Fenrik had yet to pound in to the hilt. I felt his knot press urgently against my pussy lips with each thrust and attempted to spread my legs wider, but the constriction of my pants made it difficult.

"Fenrik, I want all of you." I arched my back, ramming my ass into him, meeting him thrust for thrust. It was delicious torture to have him squeezed into me so tightly.

Fenrik used one hand to drag a calloused thumb over my nipple and snaked the other down the front of me, skating his fingers across my clit, earning him a delighted moan.

FENRIK

Tracy squeezed my cock tighter than I thought possible as I lightly pinched her nipple and flicked my finger back and forth over her sensitive bead. Even after all our time together, she was still a tight fit, but this position made it incredible. I wanted desperately to bury my knot in her, but she wasn't ready yet.

I strummed at her clit and lavished attention on each of her breasts, getting her wetter and wetter until there were slurping noises with each pump of my cock. When I thrust again, I pushed her apart just a little bit wider and admired the pink lips of her pussy as they spread to take my knot and felt it slide in finally.

"Trace, your cunt takes me so beautifully. This pussy was made for me," I growled as I watched my glistening cock disappear into her willing body. I ratcheted up the pace as I felt her delicate walls start to flutter around me with each thrust. I upped the pressure on Tracy's clit, knowing she was close to climax. She reached a hand back and grabbed me around the back of the neck, pulling me closer to her.

"I'm almost there—harder." Her voice came out ragged as she kissed down my face.

My pleasure radiated out of me. Every time with Tracy felt like it couldn't be topped. I felt my balls tighten, and stars started to swim before my eyes right as Tracy clamped down on me, screaming her pleasure, milking my cock for all it was worth. I exploded inside her warm heat, splashing cum along her walls with my knot locked inside of her as she cried my name. I thrust twice more, grunting with animalistic satisfaction at the sigh of my entire length buried deep in Tracy's swollen pink folds.

"Holy fuck, Frenrik."

"Mmmm?"

"I think we just found a way to make our afternoon strolls more romantic."

I laughed and lowered myself, wrapping my arms around her body. We slowly caught our breath as I lay bent atop her on the sun-warmed boulder. I would definitely need to remember this trail—and this boulder. I enjoyed breathing in Tracy's sweet scent as we waited to disentangle.

"Babe?" she asked after a time. "How are we going to clean up?"

Now, that is an excellent question." I pressed a kiss to her temple, thinking. "I'll remove my tunic, and we can use that."

"Won't you get cold?"

"I promise, this was worth it."

My knot softened enough for me to slide free, and I was quick to strip off my tunic and catch the cum that leaked out of her immediately. I took my time cleaning her up gently. Once finished, we both pulled up and laced our pants. Tracy turned to face me and took me by surprise by jumping into my arms, wrapping her arms around my neck, and squeezing my waist with her thighs. She kissed me, then pulled back and smiled, just taking in the sight of me and smiling.

"What is this?" I asked.

"I just really love you." She pulled me to her, tucking her face between my collarbone and jaw.

She stayed there silently; after a few moments, I realized she was shaking.

"Babe, are you cold?"

"No," she croaked, "just overwhelmed."

Oh no, she was crying. I'd never experienced someone cry after sex but that couldn't be a good sign.

"Tracy, did I hurt you?" I was, frankly, alarmed. "Was I too rough?"

"No, no," she responded quickly through sniffles. "I just…" she trailed off, tears still streaming down her face.

"Trace?"

"I just—I just can't believe…" She wiped her tears with the back of her hand. "I just can't believe I feel so stupidly lucky to have been abducted by aliens. I love my life here. I love our little tribe that has accepted me but given me space. I love our house. I love all my alien chooklings. I even love that I can tell your mom wants to ask so badly about orklings, but is respecting our privacy. But mostly… mostly… I love you." She dissolved into tears again.

Okay, well, at least this seemed to be positive crying.

"I love all those things, too," I murmured into her hair. "You are the most unexpected gift, and you make me happier every single day. I love you so much."

We held each other like that for a few moments longer as the shadows lengthened and the sun started to set. Finally, Tracy released me, putting her small hand in mine.

"You ready to go home?" she asked.

"Yes, let's go home." I tightened my fingers around her as we returned to our little cabin at the edge of the village.

EPILOGUE

FIVE YEARS LATER

TRACY

enrik and I had settled into domestic bliss. We worked the farm during the day and had sex in every position I'd imagined—and some I hadn't—at night. We found our place in the tribe, and I had even made a few close friends. It was exactly as I had hoped. The invitation to join in events was always extended but never expected. I relished our freedom and our easy commitment to each other. But when I hit my thirties I started to hear a nagging voice asking, *Don't you want to have a baby with Fenrik? Don't you want to be a mother?*

I dismissed the thought immediately. There was no way I was fit to be a mother. I had such a convoluted relationship with my own mother. I didn't want to put that on a baby—or orkling. On top of that, with Gabe, I was expected to have as many children as possible. Yet Fenrik was completely unbothered by my fear of motherhood. He said, orkling or no orking, I was his mate. But if I had a baby, it would be with Fenrik, not

Gabe. And my mother was clearly out of the picture. I got along well with Fenrik's mom, Thyra. Fenrik was an only child, and she adored him and respected his boundaries. *What a concept.*

Taking all of that into consideration, it really was down to me. Did I want an orkling—a baby? I rolled this around, weighing the pros and cons before bringing it up to Fenrik. I pictured him holding a baby, and my heart melted.

As the weeks stretched on, instead of the thought drifting out of my head, the desire became stronger. Fenrik could tell I was distracted by something, but he left me space to figure it out. We were eating roasted meat and vegetables that Thyra had taught me how to me when he finally said something.

"What's eating at you, Trace?" He stroked my thumb across the back of my hand.

I hesitated. Was now the time? I chewed my lip. "What if... what would you think about trying for a baby—an orkling?"

Fenrik dropped his fork and looked at me, eyes wide. "An orkling—you want one? With me?"

"Well, I know you've always been open to the idea but didn't want to pressure me. I have been thinking about it for a while, and all of the reasons I didn't want to have children stayed back on Earth." I fidgeted with my hands in my lap, relieved to finally tell Fenrik my thoughts, but uncertain of how the conversation would go.

"I would love to have an orkling with you, but I don't want it to open old wounds. I worry becoming a mother will remind you of your relationship with your mother and your ex," Fenrik said sincerely.

"I know. I know. But she's not here. He's not here. No one is here to watch me raise an orkling, except maybe your mom. But I have an inkling she will make an excellent grandmother. And I do not doubt you would make a fantastic father. No. I have been thinking about it for some time. And I want a baby—an orkling—with you."

Fenrik didn't even let us finish our meal. He pulled me out of my chair and hauled me up to our bedroom.

"Fenrik! I haven't even stopped drinking the tea yet!" I shouted as he threw me over his shoulder.

"Well, then, this will be excellent practice."

Fenrik pulled me into our room, which I'd redecorated in jewel tones since I'd moved in. He threw me onto the emerald duvet, ready to have his way with me. My waves fanned across the soft pillows as Fenrik raised his arms around me.

"You are sure? I know you are the one who came to me, but I want you to be certain. I don't want you doing this because you think it will make me happy," he reiterated, looking at me directly.

"I think… I think… I have always wanted to be a mother," I explained, vocalizing my truth for the first time ever.

"And all the other stuff got in the way?"

"Yes," I mumbled. "Now we are settled. We have your mom. We have the tribe. I could manage a baby. Just *one* for now, if that's okay."

"One is more than I ever expected," Fenrik whispered, crushing me into his body.

I laughed at Fenrik's enthusiasm. "I can stop drinking my tea tomorrow."

The following day, I awoke to Fenrik softly stroking along the curve of my breast. My body was already aroused, I just had to wait for my head to catch up. Then I remembered our prior conversation about creating an orkling and was immediately on the same page as Fenrik.

No birth control tea today.

I stunned him by pushing him from his side to his back and climbing atop him—I think he assumed I was still asleep. I slid my damp folds up and down his hardened cock, readying myself for him. I pulled him into a hungry kiss.

"Ohhh, Trace," he murmured, his lips not leaving mine.

I took advantage of his surprise and lifted my hips slightly before impaling myself with his cock thoroughly. Years of being with Fenrik meant I was ready to take all of him, but this time was different. We had a goal in mind.

I rode Fenrik with all of my might, both of us thrusting to meet together as deeply as possible, both of us groaning our pleasure. I tangled my hands in his hair, kissing him again hungrily as he took over with each snap of his hips until he flipped us so I was beneath him.

"I want to stuff your pretty pink pussy full of my cum," he panted.

Why does that sound so erotic?

He threw my legs over his shoulders and hammered me mercilessly. I held my breath at the overwhelming sensations. I was close to my climax, but I wanted to feel the splash of Fenrik's hot cum before I let go entirely. I felt Fenrik swell and then release into me, triggering my completion.

"Fuck," Fenrik gasped.

"Mm?"

"Just the idea of filling you with an orkling made me come harder than I ever have."

"Well, if this one doesn't stick, I am open to trying—again and again." I stroked his hair and kissed his sweaty forehead.

Fenrik looked at me as if I'd hung the moon before collapsing next to me, knot still buried deep inside.

It didn't take longer than four months of trying until Thyra was able to confirm I was definitely pregnant. We decided to keep it quiet until I was showing, but after we left Thyra's cabin, Fenrik dropped to his knees and pressed a kiss to my still-flat stomach.

"I love you so much," he whispered.

"I love you too."

EXTENDED EPILOGUE

TWO YEARS LATER

TRACY

Finally, Steve was asleep. He'd struggled since we moved him out of the crib in our room and into his bedroom. Every night, one of us read to him until he passed out. I hoped he would go to bed independently as he got older.

Although he was only two, Steve was a handful—enough for me to say one and done. After a year of no sleep, I was greeted with a year of Steve *running* at every opportunity. It didn't matter where we were, he was off, and I had to chase him and ensure he didn't end up in the lake or eaten by one of the many predators that lurked outside the village. I watched Steve breathe softly for several moments before I could leave him. I admired at his chubby light green cheeks and the shock of black hair covering his forehead. Steve might be a lot, but he was absolutely perfect. I silently rose, leaving his room, hoping he wouldn't wake. I snuck out of his room quietly to find Fenrik waiting for me on the couch in front of the fire.

"That seemed quick," he said softly as I joined him on the couch.

"Let's just hope it sticks." I sat, resting my head on his shoulder.

We sat together, watching the fire for a few moments before Fenrik nuzzled his lips into my neck.

I would be lying if I said I didn't want Fenrik. On the nights that Steve struggled to fall asleep, we were usually too tired for each other. Since bedtime had gone quickly, we had the time—and the energy. I arched, exposing my neck to him further, letting him know I was up for whatever he had in mind. Fenrik kissed down my neck and across my collarbone.

"Should we take this upstairs?" I whispered.

"How about to the bath?" he breathed, still kissing across my neck.

"That sounds heavenly."

Fenrik immediately looped his arms around me, lifting me with ease, and I let out a squeak. Even after all this time, his ability to make me feel dainty and weightless never got old. He carried me to our full washroom with a sunken tub. Fenrik stripped me of my clothes methodically, waving me off as I tried to help. Without warning, he snaked his fingers through my pussy to find my lips already damp and needy. He growled under his breath.

"In the tub," he commanded.

I didn't hesitate, almost giddy at the idea of a bath with Fenrik. I climbed into the steaming tub and relaxed in the water. My muscles were tense and tired from caring for Steve all day. He was a wild orkling, always running from one activity to the next. As I let myself float in the overly large tub, Fenrik stripped down. He pulled off his tunic and boots, then slowly unlaced his pants.

His cock was rock hard and leaking, making me want

him all the more. He joined me in the sunken tub, pulling me onto his lap.

"Steve is it for us, isn't he?" he asked as he started to press kisses down my neck.

"Is that okay?" I hesitated. "Are you okay with one?"

"More than okay." He didn't stop kissing my neck, pulling me closer to him. "I told you before we even started trying for Steve."

I was so relieved that I felt my eyes welling up with tears. I knew Fenrik would be okay with only Steve, but having him say it out loud took a weight off my shoulders.

"I love him. I love him so damn much, but I don't think I could do another," I cried softly.

"We have Steve. He is more than I could have possibly imagined—I want for nothing. I would have been happy with just you," Fenrik reassured me, rubbing my shoulders with his calloused thumbs, releasing the tension of the day as he gently massaged my muscles. I settled into Fenrik's lap, allowing him to continue the massage while feeling his erection grow and prod into my butt. He rubbed the tension out of my neck and shoulders and moved onto my back, but I couldn't take it anymore. I needed him. No matter how *sexy* sex in the bath sounded, it ended up a mess with one of us freezing. I stepped out of the tub and wrapped a large fluffy towel around myself.

"Would you like to continue this in the bedroom?" I made my meaning clear by immediately rushing from the bathroom.

I was pulling back the covers, still wrapped in a towel, when Fenrik arrived and pulled me to him. I let my towel drop to the floor as Fenrik sampled my breasts and nipples with his hands, pinching each one lightly. I groaned in satisfaction, and he lifted me weightlessly, tumbling into our shared bed. He settled me atop him, because after all these years he knew my favorite was ontop. I was happy to run the show until my thighs gave out. He slid into me effortlessly, our years together making him feel like home. We met each other, thrust for thrust, as I bent to kiss along his jaw and devour his lips. Fenrik stretched me to my limit deliciously. My lower lips were spread wide around his cock, not quite ready to take his knot. I watched as Fenrik thrust in and out of me, practically drooling at our connection. I never thought sex could be *this*. Fenrik always made sure I came twice before reaching his peak.

Fenrik slid his hand in between us, gently circling my clit until I was gasping for air. It was enough and too much all at once.

"Fenrik," I cried, "make me come."

As if it was all the permission he needed, he snapped his hips up to mine until we were simultaneously groaning at the pleasure. I steadied myself, meeting each thrust of his hips but getting lost in the feeling of his cock seeking out my most sensitive parts. Fenrik was more than I'd ever imagined, and it was easy to lose myself in his cock. But I knew he had other skills I could make use of.

"Fenrik," I mewled, "nipples!"

Fenrik didn't stop his steady thrusting but brought his mouth down to my chest. He licked and suckled each of my oversensitive nipples until I felt as if I would come on the spot. I was shaking and overwhelmed when he flipped me. I was on my hands and knees, Fenrik behind me. From this new angle, Fenrik pressed his knot into my loosened body, then sped up his urgent thrusting. He pistoned in and out of me mercilessly, our skin slapping against each other and Fenrik's knot popping in and out of me with wet, obscene noises. I moaned and cried his name, trying to keep myself quiet but knowing it was impossible. Fenrik taking me doggie style was another one of favorite positions and usually finished with me screaming his name. Now, with Steve, it was a scream stifled by a pillow.

Fenrik slowed his pace, allowing me to gather myself.

"You are absolute perfection," he breathed, wrapped around me. He pinched my nipples, earning another gasp from me.

"Please." I didn't even know what I was asking for.

Fenrik upped his pace again, massaging my breasts and pinching my nipples as my channel began to tighten. Fenrik dug into my hip with one hand while slipping the other around to find my swollen clit. He'd barely applied any pressure and I was done for. My body locked up, and my vision swam before me. I slammed face first into the pillows as I came. One, two thrusts later, I felt Fenrik expand and then jettison inside me, filling me with his warm cum.

Fenrik pulled me to him and rolled us to our sides so we could stay connected without him smothering me.

"I know we have Steve, but we've got to do that more often," I panted.

"You know my mom would love to have him overnight," Fenrik whispered, stroking my hair.

"I know. I am just not used to a mother-in-law who isn't passing judgment on my every move. My mom would have berated me for wanting time with only my husband." I curled my frame into his much larger one.

I felt his laugh more than I heard it.

"Orkin revere sex. You could tell Mom you needed three days just to fuck me, and she wouldn't blink."

"Well, now that Steve is weaned…"

"Wanna go on a little trip together, just me and you?" Fenrik asked.

"Yes," I responded without hesitation. "Tomorrow?"

Fenrik barked out a laugh. "Mom might need more notice than that, but I promise within the next few weeks. I know you loved living by the ocean, but it's too far to visit the actual ocean with Steve this little. I could take you to the ice lake. It's beautiful, but not for swimming."

"Okay, then, it's a deal." I snuggled into his chest.

It was only a week later that I stood on the edge of a clear blue lake that seemed to stretch on for miles, its waves gently lapping at the rocky shore. Fenrik was right, it wasn't for swimming, but it was gorgeous. The trees around it and the mountains it backed up to still had snow from the end of winter. I tried not to let my eyes well up, for fear they'd freeze, but it was exactly what I needed. A moment of peace with Fenrik in the presence of a never-ending lake.

I had Fenrik, I had Steve, and I had the freedom I had always longed for. Nothing could be more perfect.

LEXICON

Old Norse is a parent language to many of the Northern Germanic Languages. It is a "dead language," and there is controversy among scholars and historians about the pronunciation and use of many words.

The language used by the Orkin is a combination of Old Norse, present-day Icelandic, and some proto-Germanic terms. It is not meant to reflect any specific language, history, or people.

While some Old Norse mythology has inspired some aspects of the universe Abandoned on Niflheim takes place in, there is little correlation between what the book depicts and any original texts, myths, histories, or oral traditions of Old Norse and present-day Northern Germanic cultures.

PLANETS

Niflheim /niv-uh l-heym/ – Planet where Piper and other females have been left.

Midgard /mid'gard/ – Orkin term for earth.

TRIBES

Fýrifírar /fy:ri-fi:rar/ – Forest orkin.

Vátrfírar /va:tr-fi:rar/ – Sea orkin.

Snaerfírar /stnai:r-fi:rar/ – Orkin living in the snowy region in the highest settlements of the Fjall Mountains.

PEOPLE AND SAYINGS

Já /ya:/ – Yes.

Jarl /yärl/ – Chief or earl (masculine).

Jarlin /yärl-in/ – Chief or earl (feminine).

Kveoja /kʰvɛðja/– language spoken on Niflheim.

Elska mate /ˈɛlska/– fated mate.

FLORA AND FAUNA

Hestr /hest-err/– beasts for riding and carrying goods,

similar to horses. They have 8 legs, short curly hair, and a snout more similar to a cow.

Baldrian /bald-ree-an/– soothing herb, similar to valerian.

Chookling /²çʉklɪŋ/– a small farm animal used for meat and eggs. It has soft fur and small non functional wings that tuck tight into its body. It has a beak similar to a chicken, but eyes that are more goat like.

Kyrr /cʰʏːr/– a small woodland animal that makes its home in the base of trees. Furred, with a long fluffy tail, and bright round eyes.

Furutré /ˈfu.ɾa-treː/– Tree found in Niflheim, similar to pine.

Örn /œrtn/ – a large bird, similar to an eagle, local to the Snaerfírar.

Fjall Mountains /fjatl/ – Mountain range down the spine of the continent.

Björn /pjœtn/ – bear like predator with four eyes and two rows of sharp teeth

Skogkatt /skuːgkAt/ – large, long-haired fairy cats who live in the mountains and climb rocks

Valhnot /vahl-nut/ – Tree nut local to Fýrifírar

Grautr /græʉt-er/ – Grain like porridge served for first meal, usually sweetened with fruit and syrup

Niflfýri - forest of mist that separates the Fýrifírar from the Snaerfírar

TIME

Dagr /ˈdɑgr̩/ – day

Vika /ˈvika/ – week

Mánuthur /ˈmauːnʏðɣr/ – month

Ár /auːr/ – year

Áratugur /auːr aˈtʰʏːɣʏr/ – decade

ACKNOWLEDGMENTS

This is my first serial to be published. When my author friends encouraged me to start a serial and a Patreon I was like, *um no, no one wants that.*

Well, my patrons proved me wrong. I want to thank each and every one of you for making this possible. Without you, Fenrik and Tracy's story would only exist in my head.

Xoxo,
Jen

ABOUT THE AUTHOR

Jen has been reading for as long as she can remember. She used to get in trouble for reading *Little House on the Prairie* under her desk in elementary school. Jen's day job is advocating for adolescent mental health, something she doesn't see giving up any time soon.

Jen is married to a very polite Englishman she brought back as a souvenir from her college study abroad trip. She has identical twin mutants who make her question her sanity daily. She enjoys reading about fancy peens, napping, and watching soothing cooking shows.

She is a goth kid at heart and truly wishes she could wear platform combat boots and black nail polish on all occasions.

www.authorjeniferwood.com